MILK AND BLOOD

JADE KIM MONSEN

SIJA PUBLISHING

The characters and events in this book are fictitious. Any similarity to real persons, living or dead, is coincidental and not intended by the author.

Copyright © 2024 by Jade Monsen

The scanning, uploading, and distribution of this book without permission is a theft of the author's intellectual property. If you would like permission to use material from the book (other than for review purposes), please contact [Email address]. Thank you for your support of the author's rights.

Cover art and illustrations copyright © Rachel Sierra

Edited by David Candland Monsen and Sara DeGonia

Interior design by Jade Kim Monsen

Second edition: May 2025

ISBN 978-1-965078-00-6

1

MY STARTING POINT

It's so funny to think about now. Funny in a ha-ha way during the day and funny in a painful way at night—both are times when I'm intermittently and sporadically awake these days.

The memory that returns to me takes place in one of my mother's three living rooms. (She lives in a house that's unreasonably large for a single woman of sixty-five.) This is the living room with a large fireplace—it functions as expected but is clearly just for show, as my mother's house is located in a town that consistently archives three-digit Fahrenheit temperatures in the summer and early fall. There's a TV monitor mounted on the wall that has been turned on fewer than five times, and not one, but six doors side by side that all open to the backyard.

The small, humble bits of me understand that even this room alone is outrageous, but most of me—the part of me that often spends time with my mother and sisters drinking tea, giggling while high, playing cards or dominos, or seeing how deep we each can go in a yoga pose—also understands that this room is totally awesome.

Perhaps it's because we grew up in a smaller house when I was little and my mother had to hide me under the register below the counter of JCPenney where she rang up middle-aged women for blouses and pencil skirts.

And this night that I recall often is a night when my sisters, mother, and I had retired from cards and moved on to finding comfortable positions and throwing out random questions about the world the way children might blow bubbles. We weren't even high. This was just our nature. That night, I started. It was a strange question. Random. I had no ties to the question coming from personal desires at the time. I simply threw the question into the air.

"How long is a woman pregnant before having a baby?" I asked. There were five women in the room. Surely one of us knew, especially given one of the five women had been pregnant and birthed the other four of us.

"Six months?" Cosmic was the first to attempt an answer. Her birth name, Katlyn, which naturally transitioned to Kate in her early teen years, had fully cocooned into "Cosmic" now that she had officially reached her late thirties. She was lying on the ground. Her thick, black hair was spread across the carpet around her head as if she were an underwater goddess. Her long, dainty legs were elevated toward a ceiling that was high enough to fit three floors comfortably underneath it. When she had first told me she wanted to go by her new name, Cosmic, I had laughed immediately, and as a result, rudely. I assumed she had been to one too many yoga or psychedelic retreats. Now to think of calling her anything else sounded absurd.

"No, no. It's like a whole year." Angelica sat on a thick,

cushioned loveseat, taking her guess with a long and tired stretch and her eyes closed. When I say "sat," I actually mean sprawled. The tip of her head lay back so that her chin pointed upward, and her hair, more brittle from the dyes and blow drying, hung off the ledge of the armrest. The remainder of her body was sunk deep into the pillows. Though this was a common state of being for her when we were all home visiting our mother, it was only a state that could be reached here. It was as if she had learned to hibernate whenever she left the borders of California. Her residence now, and for the last eleven years, was in Los Angeles, where she often called me either on the brink of a panic attack or because she was breaking a diet she'd started for an upcoming audition. She never was sure which would be worse.

"It's nine months—isn't it, Mom?" My third sister, Mia, birth name Amelia, had sounded the most confident. She was still sitting up at the table, a few cards held lightly between the fingers in her left hand. She was the youngest of us at eighteen (now twenty-two) and also the one with the most promise. Her hair was pulled up into a ponytail and on top she wore only a sports bra she hadn't changed out of after her last workout. Mia was still in college and liked to talk to anyone who would listen—none in the room then would—about the surprising facts of her favorite shape: the triangle.

"I can't remember. I don't remember anything about being pregnant."

My mother was somehow a mix of all of us. She had given Cosmic her spirituality and slender physique. She had given Angelica her competitive ambition and seductive facial features: large eyes, plump lips, thick eyelashes. She had given Mia an appreciation for education and fitness that she, too, whole-heartedly exercised herself. I wonder what she gave me? Maybe her sometimes blind, sometimes unfounded confidence. Unfortunately, by this age, I had come to accept that I had inherited most of my characteristics from my father, with a hard-headedness and a knack for watching others and thinking how it could be done better. And we all shared the same family take on money: we liked it.

"You don't remember anything?" I asked.

"I remember that I didn't want to remember anything," she said.

Perhaps, that alone should have been enough to ward me off the path of pregnancy, labor, and delivery. The fact that many women have a hard time recalling the experience—though it is life-changing—should have been a signal to me that this event is something to be reckoned with. Perhaps the fact that none of my family had enough maternal intuition or knowledge to know how long a baby should grow inside our bellies should have immediately disqualified me from being able to try. Perhaps everything and everyone had actually been warning me that motherhood was not to be trifled with.

But, for whatever reason, it didn't register until—well, to say it was too late makes it sound as if I regret my decision, and a mother can't say that. It just didn't register until a later time. Which is the *now* of my life. Here, where I'm sitting up at three in the morning with the little human being I created with my husband, the baby's life and body warming my chest. This little creature hasn't let me lie my head down for slumber since their bedtime, and yet they depend on me to stay alert enough to ensure their chest continues to rise and fall until the sunrise and beyond. When I grow entirely drowsy, I remind myself that—as long as I live—I must make sure this child's breath continues.

I laugh now because I'm past pregnancy. I don't care anymore how long a woman is generally pregnant. That factoid is old and useless. I laugh out loud, startling my child, but only momentarily. It's a cruel laugh as I think about how little I knew. I only think about what I should have been asking. Like, when did sleep become an option after the baby was born? If only someone in that room would have turned and looked me dead in the eyes and told me the truth: Sleep as I knew it would only exist as a distant memory. That the only sleep involved in motherhood was in short supply and reserved only for the baby.

No matter how long a pregnancy actually was, I knew now what I didn't then: sleeping was not an option, and it often felt like it never would be.

2

LOVE SONGS, EXHAUSTION, AND CONSTANT SICKNESS

I had been pregnant for twelve weeks. Henry described it in a more sci-fi kind of way, explaining to others that I had been transformed into a vessel, carrying a tiny life form that we believe might have a conscience. Yes. He is my husband.

I had always wondered what it would be like to be pregnant. How would it feel? What big feelings would come about? What would those big changes be like? Then, along the way, I realized there were also small changes that I had never thought of before. Like love songs.

Suddenly, all of the songs that I shuffled through were no longer about my husband but about my baby. The lyrics often include the words "baby," or "darling," or "my love," and they all now referred to the hatchling inside of me. Every melody spoke to me as a soon-to-be-mother, as if the radio knew I was expecting, and I couldn't hear it any other way.

That's just one example of how my perspective had

completely changed since becoming pregnant. Music will never be the same for me.

Physical changes had also already started to occur. I made it a point to list them out to be aware of for my next pregnancy (yes, I know it's strange to think about the next pregnancy when I was barely surviving that initial first trimester).

When listing my physical ailments, my fingers had never typed so quickly. I'd come to realize (and accept) that the little piece I was writing had become a list of complaints on why I hated pregnancy. It was whining in the disguise of creative writing. At least, by writing them down, Henry didn't have to be the only audience of what I called the "Everything That Sucks About the First Trimester" essay.

Here's the deal. I'll let you know, in detail, how my baby—before even being born—often made me somewhat miserable, and I'll let the other mothers describe what a miracle pregnancy is. How about that?

Exhaustion and Constant Morning Sickness.

My two greatest foes. I had no idea how exhausting simply being pregnant would be. I didn't know days would be cut short because my desire to see any hint of a sunset would diminish, and my eyes would be completely sealed by 7:00 p.m. on a consistent basis. How could all of my energy be zapped by someone's existence who was still so . . . small? My baby was the size of a plum, so why couldn't I make it past 2:00 p.m. without napping?

I was tucked in by Henry by six or seven, too tired to feel guilty about not staying up to help around the house or spend more time with my husband. Though, I still fell asleep missing him and wishing I had more time with him each day. When he tucked me in, he put a hand on my belly and spoke to the little alien inside. Sometimes silly poems; sometimes serious, beckoning calls of love; sometimes he kindly asked for the little monster to stop making me vomit. Tears sometimes slid down my cheeks when I witnessed the two humans, one born and one unborn, converse. Oftentimes, though, I fell asleep before Henry was finished with the discourse he had started up all on his own.

With fatigue, came morning sickness. What a joke of a name for this pregnancy symptom. The audacity for it to imply that nausea only haunted the mornings. I'd felt on the verge of puking every minute of being pregnant since week four. There was always a frog in my throat, wriggling and ready to leap up out of my mouth. Water was repulsive. Kimchi disgusting. French fries only made me queasy. There was no cure. The only thing that stoked the sick away was sleep.

So, I spent the first months of my pregnancy either queasy, or drowsy, or both. There was no relief. To pass the time, I complained to Henry. I've never used my degree in English more so than I did when I was describing to my husband the most detailed recollection of my experience of constantly battling sleep or giving in to my stomach's physical reflexes. When I could no longer access my ability to communicate these treacherous symptoms in detail, I simply gave in to crying. Sometimes they were short, choked-up sobs that jerked my head back and forth. Other days they were long, dry wails that escaped my mouth while I lay my head back in surrender.

To Henry's credit, he was an excellent listener. He listened to me complain about how tired I was as he rubbed my feet in bed. He listened to me talk about how disgusting rice was as I sat over the toilet. He held me tightly when my crying spells began. He often said he wished he could be pregnant instead of me. Now that I'm writing this, I'm quite sure he wished this only so he didn't have to continue listening to my unpleasantness for ten months straight.

People told me the first trimester was the worst. People told me to hang on just a little longer. The assurance that everything would get better in just a few weeks only made things drag on, and it only made it worse when things, indeed, did not get better. They got worse in a way I could have never, ever prepared myself for.

3

FAQ OF A PREGNANT WOMAN IN HER FIRST TRIMESTER

Q: What are you craving?
A: Silence. I crave silence. Leave me alone.

Q: How are you feeling?
A: Tired. Cranky. Nauseous. And you?

Q: How many weeks are you now?
A: Twelve. A week after you asked me last time.

Q: When is your due date?
A: March. Please don't remember that.

Q: Do you know the gender?
A: Actually, no. We are waiting for the baby to come. Yes, I know that's strange.

. . .

Q: How do you know what to buy for the baby if you don't know the gender?
A: Regardless of the gender, our baby will still need clothes, diapers, blankets, etc.

Q: But what if it's a boy and you bought something pink?
A: Somehow, we'll make do.

Q: How much of your maternity leave are you taking?
A: All of it. Every last drop. (And it's still not enough.)

Q: What's your number so if I have a question about next quarter's project I can get a hold of you?
A: You don't get a hold of me. Here's my manager's contact info if you need help.

Q: Will you quit your job after maternity leave?
A: My husband will be the primary caretaker, so quitting is not part of our plan. But also, that's none of your business.

4

AVA'S SOCKS

I sit in a plain, white T and sweats. Waiting. My mind starts a slow dive into autopilot, layer by layer. A layer of attentiveness: nodding at the right times and providing direct, reassuring eye contact. A layer of smiling: showing that filling out the questionnaire I was required to fill out that asked me if I had thought about ending my life or if I felt worthless before the meeting was unnecessary. I'm good. A layer of problem-solving: preparing to ask at least two to three questions that show I'm a fully functioning adult.

My doctor walks in, but my layers have already been set. I know if I avoid going into depth in any one area, I'll be OK. I won't cry. I'll save that for later.

A week earlier, I didn't know what HCG was. I didn't know what my blood type was. And I didn't know that about **one in five women have miscarriages.** That's not what you read about on the internet when you're trying to get pregnant. My research had gone as far as the top places to purchase onesies, what half-Asian babies might look like, and how bad was morning sickness really?

My doctor asked about my support system, bringing me back to the present. Do I have a spouse? Sibling? Friend? Someone I can talk to? My layers are working. I assure her I have a supportive spouse, three sisters, and a mother who I can talk to. She nods. Then she says, "I think talking about this will help. It's healing. It's hard to talk about it, but if you can talk about it . . . It might help heal someone who can't talk about it."

I blinked, nodded, smiled. There it was again. Words. Stories. Sharing. It was what always made me feel less alone.

Over the last decade, I had slowly stopped writing— for adult reasons.

I didn't want to be that girl who was working on that book that she'd never finish.

I didn't want to look weak to my employer or coworkers when I wrote about hard things.

I didn't want to seem too wild or dark to my husband's family.

I didn't want to air my clean *or* dirty laundry in the digital world, because it's improper and what attention whores do.

I didn't want my husband to wonder, "Who the hell did I just marry?"

I didn't want to say the wrong thing and get canceled before people knew I even existed.

Over the last decade, I've slowly become paralyzed. I've slowly become afraid. I've come out of my little cave less and less. I found all of my fear, and I lost my reason to write, and I was OK with that. I was.

Then the day came when I peed on five stick things— all different brands. I was home alone, sitting and watching the double lines appear, the plus sign appear, the "yes" appear. I had never been so obsessed with staring at something covered in my own urine.

I waited until the workday came to a close and then rushed to my favorite strange pharmacy/half baby store/half ice cream shop to find something. I didn't need to rush. My husband wasn't going to be home until the next night, but I wanted to be ready. I wanted to be so, so ready.

I wanted to buy the whole store. A beetle-patterned onesie. An elephant quilt with a matching stuffed animal. Each item brought a little pain when I thought about buying it without the future father present. So, I kept it simple. I picked out the smallest pair of black-and-white striped socks. They were wrapped at the counter with white tissue paper, boxed up, and then finished off with red yarn tied into a pretty bow.

I knew it was meant to be, because my husband came home a day early to surprise me. Little did he know, I had a surprise for him. A box. He had hardly kissed me hello before I had placed the little box in his giant hands. I looked up, beaming.

"Chocolate?" he said. Any other day, he would have been right. Not today. Today was extra special.

He pulled back the tissue paper and pinched the socks softly in his hand, as if he thought if he held them too tightly, they might unravel. He looked at me. At the socks. At me. At the socks.

"What does this mean?" he asked.

It meant so much. It will always mean so much.

Henry had clambered his way to the couch, his head back, giving into the hyperventilation that came from a pure joy he had not yet experienced and that I had never witnessed in him. We created this moment together. I only bought the socks on my own.

When my husband had wiped the tears from his eyes and stood up from the couch, our lives had shifted. In the mornings we smiled, savoring the satisfaction from a good night's sleep we knew would be gone. On our walks, we talked about names, about preschool, about balancing work and a baby. We spent evenings at the bookstore in the parenting section. We purchased books for dummies; we purchased books published by doctors; we purchased books with cute illustrations that we could have finished over one cup of evening coffee. At night, I found myself tucked in early and ready for bedtime. Henry stayed up studying. He was a thirty-three-year-old college sophomore and more motivated to finish school than ever before—there was a baby on the way!

We drove north to tell Henry's parents. They cried tears of joy. Then we drove south to tell my mother. She cried tears. But they were not of joy. "Your life will be so hard now," she said, and she hugged me.

My stomach was always bloated. I was hungry when I wasn't tired and tired when I wasn't hungry. It was like one long, bloodless period the first few weeks. I complained loudly, and my husband responded with hugs, compliments, and distractions by asking me about the fantasy book I was writing.

On a Wednesday, I woke up to pinkish stains in my underwear, also known as spotting. I called Henry to tell him.

"Periods were always so weird, maybe pregnancy is too."

"Maybe. But we should check with the doctor," he said.

"Next week we should be able to hear a heartbeat. Maybe we should wait?" I asked.

"Maybe we should check with the doctor now," he said again over the phone.

I hung up and dialed another number. The questions came flooding in from the woman on the other side. *Are you spotting?* That's why I'm calling. *Are you bleeding?* No, but I'm spotting. *Are you in pain?* Well, yes, but isn't pregnancy painful? *When was the first day of your last period?* Let me see now...

Then I was in the hospital. *Let's be extra careful. Can you pee in this cup?* Yes. *Hm. Can you pee in this other cup?* Again? *Let's put some gel on your stomach.* OK. *Let's put some needles in you. We'll need some blood.* OK. *Let's put this tube inside of you.* OK.

We'll need to do more testing. Let's have you come back in a few days.

But the next morning, I'm not spotting. I'm bleeding. I'm on the phone again, and the same questions come flooding in again. *Are you spotting?* No. *Are you bleeding?* Yes, that's why I'm calling. *Are you in pain?* Very much. Is pregnancy painful? *When was the first day of your last period?* Let me see now...

I sat and waited in a different hospital. A bigger hospital. A place with better, newer equipment. A Caucasian couple sat next to me.

"It hurts so much. I want to sit on the floor," the blonde, very pregnant woman said.

"Then sit on the floor," the blonde, not pregnant man next to her said.

"No. I'm not sitting on the floor," she said—as if it were his idea.

Another couple came in. They had darker skin.

Darker than mine. This other woman was also pregnant and had long hair down past her butt. She lay on a padded bench, and her partner, with his hair in a bun, began rubbing her head.

Two women sat against a wall. They were holding an image of their baby—an ultrasound image.

"Look how *huge* she is," one woman said to the other.

I sat against another wall far away from the couples. I wished Henry was there, but more than that, I wished I knew what was happening. I wished I had gone to nursing school. I wished I knew what everyone was saying. I wished I knew what my test results meant. I wished I knew what I was looking for with all of the testing happening.

I lay down in a small room. It was dark, and there was a large screen on the opposite wall so I could watch the ultrasound as it was happening. I saw black-and-white patterns. Watching the screen was the same as watching the video games my husband played: I was sure it would be interesting if I knew what the hell was going on. I saw streaks. I saw circles. I saw colors.

"What do the colors mean?" I asked.

"The colors indicate blood flow," the man said. He continued exploring my mysterious body, and I wished that I had become a radiologist so I would know what I was looking at. I wanted to put meaning to the blips and bloops on the screen. The only thing I could discern was that when color appeared on the screen, blood was flowing, from one direction to another.

The next test required a female chaperone. A wired tube was pushed inside of my heavily bleeding cavity, and the probing continued. The discomfort increased, and my confusion remained at the same high levels.

I was left alone to change back into my clothes, and a few minutes later, a doctor with short hair and thick, circular glasses took a seat in front of me.

In so many words, she communicated that a miscarriage had been confirmed. The statistical probability was provided again as a reminder that I was not alone. One in five. She ended her short speech with an apology. I had questions. Things to say. But I only nodded.

[July 15, 2021]

Dear baby,

Henry thought you were a girl. Actually, he was sure of it. He called you Ava for twelve weeks. He talked about you like you had already met and were already friends.

When we learned we wouldn't meet you as we thought we would, he told me that you're picky like your mother (that's me), and you just didn't want the body we had started for you. I say you're like your father, a total introvert who doesn't like to leave the home.

Please take your time, but know we're ready for you when you are. We have black-and-white striped socks we're saving just for you.

Your mother, when you're ready for me,

Evelyn

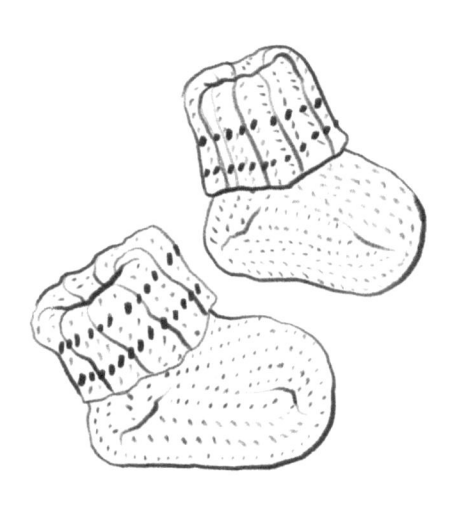

5

DÉJÀ VU

I quickly became pregnant the second time. I, being a planner, had a schedule we were already behind on when it came to when we would have our first child. I was also a woman of action. I needed to do something to feel in control. Henry was a tender and sentimental being, and because of this, I felt the miscarriage was harder on him than it was on me. Not only did I need to retake control over my life after being a first-trimester statistic but I also needed to rescue my husband before he slid deeper into a darker place I knew I would not be able to reach.

So, to put it bluntly, I seduced him.

We had had sex once since the miscarriage, and both of us regretted it afterward. I couldn't stay present when I was intimate with Henry. I couldn't help but think about the potential result of our act. A life. Maybe a loss. Sex wasn't just a pastime anymore. It wasn't just being turned on. It was a means to an end—an end we had crudely learned we had no control over. After the act, I sat up and apologized. I'm sorry, I had said. We aren't ready, are we? Henry shook his head. No.

Milk and Blood

How did I know I was pregnant for the second time? I had—I kid you not—smelled it. I sat on the toilet, peed, and my pee smelled funny and oddly familiar. I had two unused pregnancy tests in the bathroom from the first time I had excitedly bought every test in the store. I quickly made that just one unused pregnancy test left in the bathroom.

The first stick confirmed not my suspicions but my hopes. Two lines of hope also appeared on the second test I took immediately after the first. I thought back to when Henry and I had had sex. *We aren't ready, are we?* But what would become a slogan in the following weeks and months stirred in my head: ready or not, here we come ...

This was not like the first time. Being pregnant again first and foremost meant that we were painfully aware that we had something we could lose. The idea of having a miscarriage had never occurred to us during the first pregnancy. We were young, we were healthy, we figured we had nothing to worry about. So, when I was pregnant first with Ava, I purchased the socks. I handed him the wrapped box with a yarned bow. I let him guess the meaning of the gift and squealed when he came to the realization.

This time was different.

When Henry came home, I sat him down. I held his hand. His eyes were slowly traveling across the landscape of our living room. His gaze had been roaming ever since we lost Ava. His expression wasn't dark, just floating. Absent. If I had been a more sensitive person, I might have struggled to find the words. I might have waited to tell him when his face was a little brighter, the weight of the past a little lighter. But that's not who he married. He married an impatient person.

"We're pregnant," I said. Some women hate the "we" in this phrase. They can be pregnant independently, and I applaud their expression. For me and for us, there is no I in pregnancy.

Henry looked up. He stood up. He smiled, but then he walked away. After knowing him for six years, I immediately recognized what protecting himself looked like. I knew what the quiet of self-preservation sounded like, and I knew what the feeling of doubt moved like. For the next twenty-four hours, with the exception of sleeping, he kept his distance from me, and his attitude remained . . . neutral. He offered smiles from the other side of the room frequently, but they were evasive. It was as if looking directly at him would cause the smiles to disappear like some kind of optical illusion.

I regret not waiting. I sat him down and told him in the same manner that I might tell someone that everything was OK but a family member had been in a car accident. My uncertainty had gotten the best of me, and I had set the tone for the next few weeks. If I could go back, I would have held off. Not for long. Just long enough to purchase some fresh-cut flowers, a slice of cake, maybe some balloons. I could have decorated the inside of our house so that when I delivered the news, the interior would say, *Henry, this is a good thing. This is exciting. This is cause for a celebration!* But it was too late to go back and change the delivery. Now it was time to tend to the news itself.

Henry and I walked the dog. It had been three days since I told him we were expecting. We were side by side when he finally spoke about our second and newest pregnancy.

"Do you think it's Ava?" he asked.

"I don't know."

When we had first miscarried, I had listened to my husband carefully when he wondered if Ava's soul was simply not yet ready to meet us. That she had simply missed the "bus" and was waiting for the next one to jump on. Not being a spiritual person, I wouldn't normally entertain the idea. But I was vulnerable at the time, and Henry was looking to find something in me that he needed. Against my nature, I was flexible to any idea that might present the opportunity to meet Ava in this life and not "heaven," which was a place I had disregarded long ago.

I had said maybe she would come along again in the next body. Maybe she didn't like the body she was about to jump into. Maybe she would wait for the next one. I had even written a letter to her, telling her to take her time and meet us when she was ready.

Now that a few weeks had gone by since the miscarriage, to me, Ava had died. It wasn't a story I could twist into a happy ending. In this life, I had lost her, and I felt it.

He started again. "Before, when you were pregnant, I felt... like I knew it was a girl. Like I knew it was her. Now I can't tell."

"I can't either."

"But what do you really think?"

I took a deep breath. My husband knew if he asked for the truth, he would get it. I chose my words carefully.

"I think that maybe it isn't Ava. I think that Ava was in my stomach for a few weeks, and then she wasn't. Ava is her own story—a beautiful and sad one—and this pregnancy is its own pregnancy. I think maybe this is a new child with a happy beginning and middle and ending."

"So, if it's a girl, do we name her Ava?" Henry asked.

"I'm not sure," I said. "What if it's a boy?"

"Then we know it's not Ava."

And still Henry goes between the idea of the miscarriage being us simply losing the body Ava's soul was to fill and simply meeting her later in another body—or losing a body and soul altogether. I lean more toward the latter. I think we lost a baby—soul and body. That this new life will be our firstborn child, but not our first child. I don't know why I think that, but I don't think about it very much anymore—though I know Henry still does.

Though we put the conversation away for the most part, Ava was still mentioned here and there. Our doctor's appointments and ultrasounds, they were not "firsts." Still, the appointments, the routine, the symptoms . . . It all felt like déjà vu, or buying into Henry's theory, an echo from Ava. With each different doctor, technician, or nurse, we had to answer the question: Is this your first pregnancy?

Contrary to what seems to be the norm, we told our families about the second pregnancy after our first doctor's appointment. Some—perhaps most—don't like to share they're pregnant until after they get through the first trimester. Just in case. But for us, we wanted to share the good news with our families as soon as possible, and if we had to share bad news again, we would. We didn't want to have to hide our grief if it came to that again. We would share it all.

I would like to think that I approached my second first trimester cautiously. However, one does not approach the beginning of their trimester. One gets swept away in it. It's off into the unknown with a strange force that's somehow impending as it's happening. There was no caution I could take. I knew now that it was pregnancy that would choose what it took. Would it be my energy? My appetite? Or my baby? No, I did not approach my second first trimester cautiously. It floated over me, overshadowing me, and I looked at it wearily the same way I might first glance at a dark cloud on the beach I could not shake.

The simple fact was that I was now more aware of the possibility of miscarrying my baby. I went into the first trimester again, this time knowing the majority of miscarriages happen in the first three months or so. This was the most critical time. I moved slowly. I exercised safely, which meant my workouts consisted of walking and gentle yoga. I ate a wide variety of healthy foods. I took my prenatals and iron pills consistently, even if my body wouldn't keep them down for more than half an hour. And it wasn't that I didn't do these things the first time around, but I simply did them this time religiously and on tiptoe. Henry was the same. He wouldn't let me hold the dogs on the walk for fear they would jerk me too hard when they saw a squirrel. When I rubbed my arms or yawned, he appeared out of thin air with a blanket and pillow.

The doctors had said there was no reason for the miscarriage. But we did everything by the book. Just to be extra safe.

We were also acutely aware of the presence of Covid-19, the illness that made our present days "unprecedented times." Henry had gone down with Covid a year earlier when it made its first wave through our state. As much of a homebody as he was, work had still sent him out and about. I, however, had somehow managed to avoid it when my husband was sick and unable to get out of bed.

I remember it vividly. He was wearing a white T-shirt I had bought in bulk from Costco. We walked about twenty-three steps from our front door when Henry had stopped and said that was as far as he could go that day. On our way back to the front door (we had not quite made it out of our front yard), he focused on his breath. When he had made his way back to bed, he lay still, taking shallow breaths. He turned to me.

"Can you smell okay?" he had asked.

"I can smell everything," I answered.

He smiled in return. It was one of the rare moments he pressed his lips together in contentment when he was sick.

Perhaps Henry catching it early on was "lucky" for me. After that, he was adamant about isolating. He didn't want me to go through what he had gone through—and was still going through with enduring symptoms. By the time I was pregnant, we had long canceled our hot yoga memberships, cooked everything at home, and only visited the grocery stores and other necessary places in the early opening hours of the morning when they were mostly empty.

We would not let Covid ruin our plans, and despite the tragedies we faced along this strange journey, this remained true through the birth of our baby.

Still, we worried. We still spoke to the baby, hoping our voices would encourage it to continue on the path that it was on. Before, we had asked Ava, "What are you doing in there?" Now, we asked this new life, "Are you still there?"

The nausea and energy loss returned. I'd like to say I

accepted them without complaint—which was true until the second month. By eight weeks, I had returned to my ungrateful groaning, and I made sure Henry was aware of every turn of my stomach, of every drop of energy lost, and then some. Some women I confided in would remind me to appreciate the symptoms with silence, because some women can't have those symptoms at all. I bitterly bit my tongue. I had lost my first baby. So why couldn't I pout? Hadn't I earned the right? I'm sorry for those women, those parents, for the lost babies, for the never babies—just as I was sorry for Ava, and Henry, and myself. But then who would I tell the contents of my morning vomit to if I had to suck it all up and be happy about the lost breakfast?

Somehow, in a blur of symptoms, emotions, and feeling dazed and confused, we made it to the second trimester. It had been six months since we had packed Ava's socks away. The thought of having a baby felt almost too good to be true. I had to reexamine this life that was still with us. I kept second-guessing myself in the second trimester. The nausea had gone away, but the doubt had not.

"What if we don't have a healthy baby?" I remember asking Henry on one of our walks.

"I don't care if a squirrel scratches its way out of you," he said looking down at my crotch. "I will love that baby squirrel with all of my heart."

It was a strange example to use. A squirrel. Perhaps he was on the lookout for them, since it always made the dogs wild on our walks. But I will never forget when he said it. Because it was such a ridiculous thing to say, and yet at the same time, I knew—in its own odd way—it was true. I don't know if I can argue now who loves our baby more between me and Henry, but I can certainly say he loved the baby *before* I did. Though there's some shame in my fears of our baby's health that may cause some to think less of me, I hope it makes them also think more of Henry.

And I can't stress that last part enough. When the second trimester came, my physical ailments did grow milder. But it was just a trade for a wreck of emotions. I had some rather intensely embarrassing outbursts. I cried like the world was ending. I often tried to fabricate loose reasons to justify the meltdowns, but I was never quite sure why the tears came. Henry would never admit it, but they scared him. I could see it in his eyes. Fear. However, he never looked annoyed or irritated. Only afraid. Of what I was doing or of what he wasn't able to, I'm not sure.

In the third trimester, my body and mind were somewhat quieter, though still stirring. I went between adoring how small the little outfits were that my baby would somehow fit into to wondering how I would work full-time (with six weeks of maternity leave) and the baby needing me in their first days, weeks, months, and okay, years. I felt like my youth had suddenly been sacrificed to make way for my baby's youth. That my body was, in a way, being sacrificed for my baby's body. Yet, I never despised or envied my future child. I only wondered about this trade.

I wondered if I had what it took to remain myself and raise the child. My mother had said she forgot who she was, and she forgot about taking care of herself when her kids came into the picture. She was an excellent mother. Would I grow to be a mediocre mother if I tried holding onto my work, my writing, and my time to exercise and nourish my own body? I kept telling myself it was a balance that I would need to keep. But how do we balance ourselves when our baby would become our everything in an instant? How can you not be absorbed by such a relationship?

I doubt Henry had these worries. I'm sure, like his own father, he was born to be a father. He was born to teach, to protect, to love. I saw it in him when he was with his niece and nephew, but I also saw it when he tended to the garden in the front yard, to our little house in Salt Lake, to the spiders he caught and let outside. I don't think he risked losing himself. If anything, he would only find himself in the next steps of his life. In fatherhood. Maybe that's why he couldn't wait. He talked about the baby and to the baby all of the time. He'd already told me what he would teach our child, what he'd support them in (everything), what kind of parent he hoped to be...

I would rub my belly and say to my baby aloud, "Even if I'm just an average mother, your father is five stars, my love. You've lucked out there. And yes, I'll take some credit there. I chose him. Did good, didn't I?"

6

LINEA NIGRA

The dark line divides
    The center of my body,
    The portal to your soul.

Your creation cuts me
    In half;
    Your existence makes me whole.

7

THE OTHER

Sure. I was aware of pregnant people before I was pregnant. I was aware, but this awareness was coming from second- or third-hand sources. For example, I was aware that I should give up my seat if I was on the bus or train when they walked in because of a sign near a seat that told me so. I had also seen on TV that expecting women had strange cravings and liked to balance plates and bowls of food on their belly. It was rather comical to me really.

But I had learned nothing of their discomfort, needs, and symptoms from themselves, and I had learned nothing from actual pregnant women because I was never around them. See, none of my friends were ever pregnant, and if they became pregnant, well, we just stopped talking. I'm not sure if it was me or them. Or both of us for different reasons. I know I never reached out. I never asked about their pregnancy, and quite frankly, it was because I never cared.

I look back and see a pattern. A friend became pregnant, and then that was the last I heard of them. It was like a puppy that was taken to "the farm" to live out the rest of their lives. I knew they were still alive, because I would see photos of them and their partners and babies on social media.

It would start with the snapshot of their baby lying on their back, feet up, and a black felt board or some other crafty worded display indicating one month of their life. I would see this as I scrolled through my newsfeed, and I would think, "Oh, right. They had a baby. Cute." Then onto the next image, which would be a friend on a luxury vacation with friends and money I didn't have, camping in the Uinta Mountains with an appreciation of the outdoors I had never learned. Or perhaps the next image would be a sponsored post of the world's most innovative sports bra.

So, I had to have had *some* idea of what would happen once I made the announcement. My friends would be social connections that made their support known through double taps and using their "recently used" emojis. When I would post a photo, they would give me three red hearts in the comment section, and that would be the totality of our friendship.

But I had naively thought it would be different because I was very, very close with my family. My family was different. My mom was like a sister. My sisters and I were known among crowds as "thee sisters." My siblings and I were in our twenties and thirties, and we drank tea and played games. From across state lines, we Facetimed often back and forth. Whoever had more juicy stories would be the first one to call. Our group message was filled with chatter throughout the day, every day.

This would be no different, I thought. They would get to learn about all of the things I was curious about when it came to pregnant women—the physical changes, the cravings, the labor—all through me. I would let them ask questions, and I would tell them interesting facts. We would laugh at my growing belly and giggle at my belly button when it fully transitioned into an "outie." Or so I thought...

You may have noticed from the moments I became pregnant both times, I've mentioned my family very little. This was not an accident.

In college, I studied English with an emphasis in Gothic Fiction. We read *Frankenstein*, *Dracula*, *Jane Eyre*, and *The Picture of Dorian Gray*. A theme that was common throughout gothic literature was "Otherness" or "the Other."

In Webster's dictionary, *Otherness* is defined as "the quality or state of being other." Other is defined as, "being the one remaining or not included," or, "disturbingly or threateningly different."

This is what I became in my family, and I had not anticipated it. I called up often, and even the dial tone of Facetime felt forced. The expressions on their faces were always bored, and mine frozen. I had wanted to tell them what a linea nigra was, and Cosmic—not quite reluctantly but hesitantly—told me about the three different people she had had sex with on three different days in the same week. When I showed Angelica the low of my belly beginning to plump (upon her request), she said, "Ewwww." When I told Mia I was feeling nauseous, she said, "Cool," though to be fair, I think she was finishing up her homework while we were on our call.

To also be fair, I didn't know how to respond to their life stories. I didn't have interest to live vicariously through them when they talked about ayahuasca retreats. I didn't care to speculate if the girl who had given my sister the wrong number had done it on purpose. I even felt like Mia, who was closest to my strange, increasingly domesticated life, gave me nothing I cared to work with when she mentioned her college classes, frat parties, and summer backpacking plans in Europe.

I was somehow just as disinterested. But I still desired to be close. After experiencing the weirdness and wanting to shrink back, I decided to force myself to not disappear from the landscape of my family. I made a deal with myself. I would call each sister once a month to check in with them. This way, I would know I was reaching out but wouldn't be bothering them if they were uncomfortable or bored. One call a month was cordial. I was careful not to dial their numbers more often for fear I was scaring them with what I thought would draw them in: a new chapter none of us had ever lived yet.

I was careful to pick my topics with them even around pregnancy.

Cosmic was uninterested in children because she was uninterested in settling down. She blew where the wind took her, and children would make her too heavy to get swept away. When we chatted, she would ask questions about my body and explain how my chakras worked. "Though I'm not sure how that changes when you're pregnant," she added with her head tilted on the screen.

In past conversations, Angelica had been vocal about wanting to get married and have kids. I thought that our calls might turn out to be the most pleasant since we had had that in common now—but I couldn't have been more wrong. In fact, talking with her was the most challenging. When I brought up my pregnancy, she would either change the subject so abruptly that I was sure she hadn't even heard what I had said, or she would share a gruesome story about some of her friends' past pregnancies that usually involved uncontrollable weight gain, uncontrollable bowel movements during labor, or uncontrollable emotions that ended in divorce.

When I asked about her life, it was filled with more auditions, more acting classes, and more men. And after listening to her career and dating woes and triumphs, I too failed in being able to ask the right questions in hopes of feigning interest.

Mia and I weren't big talkers on the phone. We lived in the same city and often spent quality time together, in person. But she had classes in the morning, work in the afternoons, and a new boyfriend in the evenings. Naturally, I saw her rarely. Our interactions were polite and without any of Cosmic's disconnect from sexual beings and pregnant bodies or Angelica's many friends' pregnancy horror stories—but they were without depth. When I was twenty-three, I didn't care about heartburn after long naps either. So, we kept our moments short.

My mother called every week. She would start our conversations with a leading question: "Are you not feeling good right now?" "Isn't it so difficult being pregnant?" "Is the financial stress more than you need right now?" "Is Henry not helping as much as you thought he would?" Before we could start a conversation, I already felt exhausted. The positive side to the calls with my mother were that because her questions were so negatively positioned, my stubbornness forced me to fight the other way: "I'm actually feeling better than last week." "It's difficult, but still really fascinating." "We've budgeted and planned for this. We're doing well." "Henry has gone above and beyond every day. He's never missed an appointment."

I had confided in my mother that my connection with my sisters wasn't the same. As different as we had always been from one another, we always came together. I had always felt this special bond with them that many a friend had confessed they envied. My mother told me, "There. There. Your sisters don't know what you're going through, but they love you. They're there for you. Now, how much has your face swollen since you've become pregnant?"

Immediately announcing my pregnancy, I knew I had lost all of my nonparent friends. Halfway through my pregnancy, I had accepted the unexpected loss of my sisters as well. By the final month, I saw myself clearly as "the Other". I was thirty-nine weeks and four days pregnant when I went into labor. My monthly calls to each sister had been the only thread that seemed to remind us that we were, in fact, sisters. In those thirty-nine weeks—the equivalent of about ten months—I never received a single call from any of my sisters.

I had never felt more alone. By the time our baby came, I considered my relationships with my sisters all but evaporated. It broke my heart that my celebration of my new family was so small. When the baby came, I decided to end my monthly outreach for the time being and was left to stir on what I had read once in college from Mary Shelley's *Frankenstein*: "It is true, we shall be monsters, cut off from all the world; but on that account we shall be more attached to one another."

8

GUEST CONTRIBUTOR

My dad died of cancer when my firstborn was two weeks old. I was in mourning. Grieving. Exhausted. I don't know who took care of my baby, but it wasn't me. I can't remember the first five months of my child's life, and I'll never get that back.

No one talks about when life happens when becoming a mom happens. Having a baby is so hard, but what happens when you're going through another traumatic event at the same time? Add guilt to loss, and that will sum up my experience as a mother. I'm going to spend the rest of my life making it up to my little Chrissy.

9

THE SEAWEED SOUP (미역국) RECIPE—A PLAY IN ONE ACT

Characters:

할머니 (my mother, soon-to-be grandma.)

Evelyn (me)

Henry (Henry)

Scene I

Evelyn is in her kitchen. She's just finished folding the laundry with the help of her husband and has now moved on to the dishes. She hasn't showered and is disappointed that the new maternity yoga pants she bought are riding up her vajayjay.

Henry is reading on the couch, waiting for the NBA playoffs to start.

할머니 *on the other end of the line has just worked off the last of her protein shake at the gym and is on her way to eat lunch with her friend. Her new eyelash extensions were applied just last night, so her eyes water a little more than normal. She dials her daughter and puts the phone on speaker for the duration of her call in her car.*

Evelyn
    Hi, Mom.

할머니
    Hi! How are you feeling?

Evelyn
    Fine. A little tired.

할머니
    Are you third trimester yet?

Evelyn
    No. Next week.

할머니

Okay. So, I have this recipe.

Evelyn
Okay...?

할머니
It's for seaweed soup. Miyeok guk.

Evelyn
That's really nice, but Mom, I don't really feel like cooking.

할머니
You have to make it and eat it.

Evelyn
Why?

할머니
The seaweed is slimy, right?

Evelyn
I guess...

할머니

When you eat slimy seaweed, it will make you more slippery, and the baby will slip out. No problem!

Evelyn

...

할머니

I did it for all of my babies.

Evelyn

I thought you couldn't remember being pregnant.

할머니

I remember seaweed soup, and all of my babies came fast.

Evelyn

OK, OK. What's the recipe?

할머니

You have a pen and paper?

Evelyn

Yes. How do I make it?

. . .

할머니

Are you ready?

Evelyn

Yes!

할머니

OK. First you soak dried seaweed overnight.

Evelyn

OK. How much seaweed?

할머니

How much? Just you know, a few handfuls.

Evelyn

Mom...

할머니

Just two handfuls. What feels right.

Evelyn

OK. Soak seaweed.

할머니

Six to ten hours.

Evelyn
OK. Soak some seaweed for six to ten hours.

할머니
In the morning, just like when you soak beans, the seaweed will be bigger. Much bigger. So, make sure there's a lot of water.

Evelyn
OK.

할머니
Then, you have to wash it. Because it's from the sea, and that's where all of the garbage is, and where people swim.

Evelyn
Ha-ha OK...

할머니
So, really squeeze it and wash it. For at least two minutes. You have to get the salt out and the sea off.

Evelyn

OK.

할머니

Then put sesame oil in the pot for the soup on low heat.

Evelyn

How much sesame oil?

할머니

How much? This is your favorite soup. You've seen me put it in.

Evelyn

Yeah, but Mom, I wasn't paying attention.

할머니

Just put enough to spread around the pot.

Evelyn

... OK.

할머니

Then put beef in.

. . .

Evelyn

How much beef?

할머니

Well, how much beef do you eat? You're the pregnant woman.

Evelyn

You're the one who wants the pregnant woman to cook!

할머니

I would cook if you lived closer!

Evelyn

Mom, where you live, they don't even sell seaweed. Anywhere.

할머니

OK, OK. So, after soaking seaweed, sesame oil, put pieces of beef in. You remember how the beef looks. So cut it like that.

Evelyn

OK.

. . .

할머니

Then lots of garlic. Maybe six of them.

Evelyn

OK.

할머니

Then amino acid. Don't use soy sauce. Only amino acid. It's healthier.

Evelyn

OK, OK. How much?

할머니

Just until the soup is the right color.

Evelyn

Mom.

할머니

You should know! You watched me make this soup one hundred times.

Evelyn

How do you not know?

. . .

할머니

One-eighth cup. OK? One-eighth cup amino acid.

Evelyn

OK.

할머니

Then lots of black pepper, and no salt. Because the seaweed is from the sea!

Evelyn

Right.

할머니

You always liked extra black pepper.

Evelyn

That's right.

할머니

Then mix it all up. Only use a wooden spoon. Don't use anything else. Wood is good. Cook until meat is brown. Then put water in it.

Evelyn

... Do you know how much water?

. . .

할머니

Well, how much soup do you want to eat? Four to five cups usually is what I put in maybe. Around there. Boil the water. Then cook on low for thirty minutes, and then it's good. You eat it for your third trimester, and the baby will just slide out.

Evelyn

Sound logic.

할머니

Huh?

Evelyn

OK. That sounds good. Thanks, Mom!

할머니

I think it's going to be a girl. I had only girls. So, I know.

Evelyn

Maybe.

할머니

OK, I have to go to lunch with Rita now.

. . .

Evelyn
OK. Bye, Mom.

할머니
OK. Love you. Poor Evelyn. Love you.

Evelyn
Love you.

Click

Henry
Where are you going?

Evelyn
To the Korean supermarket.

Henry
Oh, I'll come with. Can we get those pickled turnips that I like?

10

DELIVERY

We had known this moment was coming for months. We had taken classes; met with doctors; gained certification in infant and toddler CPR; read countless books by pediatricians, labor and delivery nurses, and scientists; spoken with others who were already "on the other side"—and it didn't matter.

We weren't prepared.

It's hard to prepare for something that can be so different from one person to the next, from one baby to the next, from one family to the next. That's actually why Henry and I didn't go to the hospital with a birth plan, despite every other blog post insisting we should. We had an idea of some of the things we wanted, and they were all things that were already standard practice at our hospital. By default, our hospital:

- Supported breastfeeding in multiple ways to ensure the mother was given every opportunity to establish breastfeeding first.
- Prioritized vaginal delivery over C-sections and

preferred C-sections only be performed if they were absolutely necessary.

- Focused on skin-to-skin contact as early as possible and for as long as possible.
- Offered flexibility in medication to manage pain, from full-fledged drugs to heat, water, and motion.

In short, the hospital's preferences were our birth plan.

It was our last scheduled doctor's appointment when the doctor discovered I didn't have enough amniotic fluid for the baby, which increased the risk of having a stillborn. My water must have broken or torn with a leak, but I hadn't noticed. The realest part for me was when our doctor, Sandy, paused, looking at her monitor, and asked, "Did you just feel that contraction?"

I shook my head.

Then she said, "You're in the early stages of labor. Today is the day. Do you have a bag ready?"

We were able to stop by the house to collect our prepacked bags. Mia was able to stop by and take a photo and give us hugs. When we headed for the hospital, Mia waved us off before she went on her own adventure. Disneyland with her boyfriend.

"Couldn't they have picked any other time to go to Disneyland?" I asked as we drove away.

"You're the one who doesn't want anyone else in the hospital for the birth," Henry reminded me.

When we arrived at the hospital, we were ushered straight to the emergency labor and delivery area. Before, I had come to the hospital feeling sick or for an appointment. It was different coming to have a baby. The front desk had asked if I needed a wheelchair. I declined. I was too nervous to sit, and I could walk just fine. The nice lady escorted us to the women's center, having us take the elevator. It felt silly to use the lift to go up one floor, but she insisted.

A receptionist led us to an available room. Our doctor had called ahead, and they had been expecting us. On our way up, I thought about all of the movies I had watched where the woman's water broke and chaos ensued. Here I was, I didn't even notice when my water had broken, and there truly had been little chaos up to this point. There were no gushing waterfalls from my skirt, no panicked phone calls to the posse, no rushing and running and screaming. It was just ordinary. Even though we were checking into the emergency labor and delivery area that literally had the word "Emergency" before labor and delivery, it was still ordinary. Almost reverential.

The room was large and filled with hospital-grade machines and . . . things. I couldn't tell you what they were. Just foreign, hospital-like machines I had always seen in TV shows. Wires and beeping screens displaying information communicated by different monitors that were not yet hooked up. There was a picture hanging on one wall of red rock—canyons from somewhere in Utah. I changed into the hospital gown I was given. I was also instructed to wear a stretch wrap around my stomach. I had no idea what it was for, but I was sure I would find out.

It felt like things were happening fast. Our dedicated nurse came in and introduced herself. She asked why we were there and if we had any questions. Henry and I gave her short explanations, understanding she was simply doing her due diligence. Then she proceeded to explain what she would be doing next: checking vitals, inserting an IV, etc. She continued to ask questions about our delivery, with the big one being whether we still wanted the gender to be a surprise. Henry and I both confirmed the notes.

"Who wants to announce the gender when the baby comes? OK, and does Dad also want to cut the umbilical cord?" She went on to ask and discuss other medical questions. Family history, allergies, medications, etc.

While she asked these questions, she had strapped a few monitors around my belly, securing them by placing them under the elastic wrap I had pulled up over my protruding stomach. One was to monitor the contractions as they came and went. One was to monitor the baby's heart rate. There was one more, but I forget what it was. It's funny how fast I forget these things now. Maybe my heart rate? They were stuck on with the same gel they used for ultrasounds and then tucked away under the wrap.

We had a student come in to ask a few questions. They were similar to the medical questions regarding family history, possible risks, etc. She also asked about our previous pregnancy. I remember her saying that she understood we'd had a pregnancy previous to this one and asked if there were any complications.

I answered: "Yes, we miscarried." But I realize now she was wondering if there was anything that happened to have caused the miscarriage—which there wasn't. It was just some weird fluke. Just another statistic. I began to trip on my words. Henry had started talking, and I lay back, relieved.

At that point, I suddenly felt my throat go dry. I asked for water. Then I turned to Henry and told him I was feeling lightheaded. My vision started to blur, and everyone around me started to sound like they were underwater. I'd never had a panic or anxiety attack, but I wondered if that was what I was having. I asked Henry if that was what I was having. I felt so hot. I was starting to sweat. The nurse went to get a Gatorade, and the student left to alert the resident doctor.

I took a few sips of the Gatorade. Henry was patting my forehead with a wet towel the nurse had given him. My vision came back. My hearing cleared up. My overheating had cooled to a cold sweat. I looked down, and the IV had been inserted into my left arm. The nurse had tried on my right arm but apparently had to try again on my other arm. She had also drawn a few tubes of blood. For some reason, this comforted me. It wasn't that I was having a panic attack thirty minutes into this new adventure—I was simply lightheaded from the blood draw and IV.

We had been here all but thirty minutes, and I was already on the verge of passing out. How the fuck was I going to have a baby?

At that point, the resident OB had come in. She asked about my lightheadedness and then proceeded to explain what was happening. It was maybe the third time I was hearing that I was going to be induced with a balloon. This balloon would cause mild cramping when it came out, and when it came out, it would mean my cervix was dilated to three centimeters (ten centimeters being the goal). They would also be placing a pill inside my vagina that would help open my cervix during the course of four hours. If my cervix was not opening as needed, they could insert another pill after four hours to continue the induction.

Besides a C-section, being induced was the second thing on my list that I didn't want to happen when I had a baby. But it *was* happening, and that, my friends, is how it goes.

She asked if I understood why we were doing this (low amniotic fluid), and she also asked if I had any questions or concerns. I always asked Henry if he had any questions or concerns. But we both knew with low amniotic fluid levels, the risk of stillborn was increased, so we were determined to move forward. I wouldn't have been so confidently inclined if our baby wasn't at term (which is thirty-seven weeks or more), but we were at thirty-nine weeks and four days. It felt like good timing, and in our OB appointment earlier that morning, we had already been discussing an induction if the baby were to not come at the forty-week mark.

The next step was checking to see how far my cervix was dilated. They offered me a few pain relievers (fentanyl, laughing gas, etc.), all of which I declined. Checking my cervix didn't sound very scary or painful. I had no idea how this was done, and lo and behold, it was done in a very old-fashioned manner.

The doctor put on gloves and inserted her fingers into my vagina. To reach the cervix to see how dilated it was, she had to insert her fingers, hand, wrist, and then some, *very* far in. It went from uncomfortable to painful very quickly. She paused and let me breathe and then waited for my call for when she could continue. She let me know I could tell her to pause at any time. But I just wanted it done, so I just kept wincing in pain and breathing awkwardly without saying anything.

It was quite painful, but not totally terrible. Henry held my hand. He told me he was proud of me. That I was incredible. And I kept thinking about how badly I wanted to see him hold our baby. That and *damn-damn-damn* this is uncomfortable and painful and stupid. It's 2022. Did we not have a better way to check a fucking cervix?

What was more terrible was that when she pulled her hand out, she verified that we were about half a centimeter dilated. For some reason, I had been convinced I was halfway to ten centimeters already. It was discouraging to know we had so far to go, but the nurse had assured us it was quite normal, and we'd be there soon enough.

Ten centimeters. It was such a short length, generally speaking. Put it into this context, and it felt like an impossible distance.

Then our dedicated nurse left with the doctors to prepare the pill and balloon for my cervix. The room went quiet. We were finally alone for the first time since arriving at the hospital. I looked at Henry and began to cry. He sat near me and held my hand. I distinctly remember him leaning forward, his eyes watering as he said, "What is it? Talk to me. I'm here. Talk to me." But I didn't have anything to say.

I was overwhelmed. I was scared. I was going into labor through induction and with a balloon—the one method besides a C-section I most wanted to avoid. (Who wants a balloon to stretch out your cervix?) I was expecting my water to break. For the contractions to come. Instead, we were there, beckoning labor to come, and it felt so . . . unnatural. It was like I knew it was going to hurt because we were taking the baby before my body was ready to give the baby away.

But Henry. Just hearing his voice: "Talk to me." I just let the words flow, which were hardly full sentences, and he listened, and we sat in our emotions together. He watched me in that moment more intently than I had ever been watched before, and I felt his heart flicker every time I held my breath or my chest fluttered. We were there together, and we were having this baby.

"It's a birthday balloon for our baby," Henry had said smiling. "That's what the balloon is for."

The nurse came in and saw us together. Me, crying. She was very sweet and asked me to just tell her all of my thoughts. What was I feeling? I just continued to cry, and she said that crying was okay. The baby was okay. Everything was okay. Her name was Abby. During the course of the next few hours, I learned that she was twenty-two and had dated her boyfriend for three years. Her job was the best birth control (I did not laugh when she made this joke). I wanted to ask if that was birth control just for now, and did she want to have kids later, but I decided not to. What business was it of mine?

Before inserting the pill and balloon, they offered me pain medication again. It was not annoying or pushy—especially because I let them know I really just wanted to stay flexible and know what my options were at all times. I declined. This time around, a different person was placing these things vaginally, and it wasn't as painful, despite it being even more invasive and, of course, they were leaving things up there in the tiny little opening in my cervix. I think the first time the doctor went in, it had stretched me out some. The balloon was inserted as well as the pill. When this was done, the doctor said I was actually about one-and-a-half-centimeters dilated, which was a nice little consolation prize. The next steps were to wait. Four hours and they would come back and check again.

But for the time being, the nurse said my contractions were so frequent that they couldn't even give me Pitocin if I had wanted it—which I didn't. (It was the third thing I didn't want to be a part of my labor experience. This wasn't because of research or statistics; it was because my friend had told me Pitocin had caused her contractions to become so strong that her baby couldn't breathe. She immediately was given something else to counteract the Pitocin. It was a single story that had stayed with me so that when the nurses said I wouldn't be getting any Pitocin anytime soon, I felt relieved.)

My contractions continued to get stronger while still happening every minute. The frequency was too fast to birth a baby and would be dangerous because it wouldn't let the baby breathe. However, the nurse didn't seem alarmed and said she would wait for them to slow down and get stronger before anything else.

The four hours passed. We ate a meal provided by the hospital. Turkey sandwiches! I hadn't had a turkey sandwich in ten months. The nurse assured me it was okay when I hesitated when she asked me what kind of sandwich I wanted. Henry got one too. I didn't feel hungry and thought it silly to order food at a time like this, with a balloon up my v-hole. But as soon as I took a bite, I finished the entire thing, chips and all. My contractions also didn't slow down, though they started to get stronger.

A man came in. He talked for what seemed like fifteen minutes straight about the benefits and risks of the different pain medications. We explained we wanted to be flexible and signed waivers and forms that gave our consent for the drugs (an epidural, basically) if needed. That way we didn't have to do so later on if I was in pain and wanted them. It was definitely nice to have everything signed in advance.

The nurse came in a few times to check on us, and she explained that I was having uterine tachysystole, a thing where I was having more than five contractions in ten minutes. Pitocin still wasn't an option (which I was still happy about), but there was nothing to worry about because I was still not dilated. At this point, I had already pooped twice. It felt very similar to how I have to poop when my period cramps get bad. I was relieved, because I wanted as much out of my system before intensive labor started—though I still felt like I had a lot in there I wanted out. But I took what I could get—or rather got rid of what I could.

The nurse then said she would check the balloon. She tugged on it with my legs spread like a butterfly and said, "No, not yet." Four hours of waiting and tachy contractions, and not even three centimeters? It was pretty devastating.

At this point, we ordered another couple of sandwiches. I devoured mine again, even though, when ordering, I thought I wouldn't touch it. Another hour or so passed, and the nurse came back to check the balloon. I wanted Henry to sleep, but I knew he didn't want to miss anything. So, I woke him. I lay back and spread my legs. Henry held my hand, and she tugged. The balloon flubbered out! It was the strangest feeling. Like a huge fish had floundered out between my legs, and it made the weirdest sound to go along with it. The nurse said I was three centimeters open, and at this point, she said I was still doing fine with contractions on my own. Then she left me to rest again, though resting was not what was happening.

I realized after the balloon had been pulled out that my contractions were picking up in strength. They still continued to be one minute apart—Henry and I watched them on the screen as they came. But the pain suddenly amplified. I quickly went from being able to eat a sandwich and chat to not being able to speak. The pain reached the same levels as the worst period cramps I've ever experienced. I tried to breathe through them. I didn't do a great job. The nurse taught Henry how to do pressure points on my knees, and he got up *every minute* to push on my knees and offer a little relief. Having Henry holding strong onto my knees seemed to give me something to anchor onto other than the pain—until the pain increased even more, and I started to vomit from the intensity.

At this point, Henry became my champion. He was up and pressing my knees, rubbing my hands, telling me how exciting it was that we were going to meet our baby. He asked about the pain, about how he could help. He told me he loved me over and over again, and I felt my love for this man grow to exponential amounts that I wish I could have better communicated to him at the time. The only thing I could do was look teary-eyed at him and take a few breaths in between my whining.

That's when I asked Henry to tell the nurse I wanted to talk about pain management. She came in, and I asked her what getting an epidural would look like and what it would do. She simply smiled and said, "It would take away the pain."

At this point, my cervix was checked again. I was five centimeters dilated. That finally felt like progress. Henry was smiling, and that put me more at ease. I was happy to see him relieved.

We work off of each other's energy like that. Not just then in that situation but always. When I'm stressed, he feels it. When I'm happy, he feels it. And I feel the same for him. We're forever reactive to each other's emotions and well-being—which means we're so connected and close, but it can also be tough in a situation like that, where I was only feeling pain, stress, and fear. I see it transfer, and it's hard to keep it from spreading to the love of my life.

The pain was terrible. I told Henry I wanted the epidural, and so he let them know. It took a while for them to come in. Maybe it wasn't too long, but I was in so much pain that I was getting impatient. Finally, a new doctor arrived. She took out a tray and, without focusing on it, I knew there were many instruments on it that I would not want to see. I didn't have enough time to be afraid of the needle, but still, somehow, the fear was greater than the pain. There's just something so vulnerable about leaning forward and letting someone stab you in the back with a giant needle.

The anesthesiologist rolled the band I was wearing up on my belly. She cleaned my back with something cold. Then a table was placed in front of me.

"It's like cat in cat/cow in yoga," the doctor said.

My new nurse (Abby had left hours ago) Grace now made sure I was doing what I was supposed to.

I leaned forward on a table while sitting on my bed. I saw Henry's face not where I expected. It was under the table, his head poking out. I saw his eyes, waiting for me to meet them. He was kneeling on the ground so he could put pressure on my knees during contractions. While turning, walking, rolling, and sitting, he had not left my knees alone. I smiled at him. I was in pain. I was afraid. And in this moment, more in love with my husband than I had ever been.

So, with pressure on my knees from Henry, I sat as still as I could—still shaking from the contractions that were coming every minute. They refused to slow down. My entire body was trembling from the pain—maybe a little from the shock of just the entire situation as a whole. My teeth were chattering. Up until that point, I had tried to keep my palms open to help me breathe and stay relaxed. I finally closed my hands over the table, gripping as hard as I could to brace for pain and to try to keep my body still through contractions.

"Don't reach back," the anesthesiologist said.

Why would I reach back? I asked rudely in my head. "OK," I said out loud.

"Tell me when your contraction is coming down," she said. Then she kept reminding me not to reach backward.

Funnily enough, I can't remember the pain from the epidural. I'm guessing it was like any shot. Perhaps I was just in so much pain from labor that I didn't really process the epidural. But what I do remember is that I was really scared. I know there are rational reasons to be scared of the epidural. A big needle (I still don't know what it looks like). Something intense happening around a very vulnerable area, the spine. Scary stuff happening behind me where I can't see. Side effects. Things could go wrong. There were plenty of rational reasons to be afraid, but I remember being afraid more through my emotions. For irrational reasons. And so, I can't recall the pain, but I can recall that strange, indescribable fear.

Leaning forward, I felt like I was trusting another human being with what really felt like my life. I know that's a bit extreme, but I think this fear really came from not trusting people with important things. I've always had a hard time with it, and yet, here I was curled up over a table, a nurse trying to keep me still, Henry underneath the table trying to keep my attention on him, a doctor administering a heavy drug into my spine. There were a lot of people I had to trust for things to go right—and I wasn't ready.

Thank god that didn't matter. Trust or no trust, the nurse was great. The anesthesiologist was also an expert. And Henry, well, I already trusted Henry. My knees had never been more attended to.

After the doctor was finished, there was a tube or wire strapped on top of my right shoulder. The doctor and nurse both assured me that it was staying put and I could lie down again. They asked me to wait twenty minutes for the pain to go away and assured me they would be back to check in soon.

My feet began to tingle. I could still move my legs. My thighs began to tingle. As the contractions came, I still felt pain in the beginning, as I was waiting for the drug to set in. I instinctively asked Henry to stop pressing on my knees but to simply grab the tops of my thighs and squeeze. Hard. This really helped for some reason. It just helped me focus on something, a firm, grounding sensation.

Next, the nurse put a urinary catheter in my body, taping a tube to my leg. I felt a strange sensation but no pain (to my relief). After having to get up to pee every fifteen to thirty minutes for the last ten months, it was actually nice to not have to worry about my bladder for the next few hours.

The pain did start to leave my body. Except, it was remaining very intense on my right side. My stomach and back. It almost felt worse, because the sensation was so focused in one area, like I was getting stabbed. Twenty minutes went by. Then thirty. I could hardly move my right leg from the numbness, but I could easily lift my right. It wasn't working on one side. We had a little button hooked up to the epidural that I could push every fifteen minutes to give me a "boost" of the drug. We used it. It didn't work on my right side. I told Henry, "It's not working." Something was wrong.

We brought the nurse in. By instruction, I lay on my right side to help the epidural travel to that side. It definitely helped, but it was still very painful. I knew the contractions were still just ramping up for active labor and then would get even more painful in the pushing stages, so I was scared I wouldn't have the relief I needed before it was go time.

We also had to monitor the baby more closely. Moving to the side could be helpful but could also make "baby unhappy," so we kept a close eye on their heart rate as I waited on my side. Still no relief. I let the nurse know. She wanted to wait longer to see how it would be on my side after thirty more minutes had passed. This is when Henry spoke up, and I'm really glad he did—I couldn't. I was in too much pain. "The pain is still very intense on her right side. We need to get the anesthesiologist back in here now. Not in thirty minutes."

My husband, I thought lovingly. My fucking advocate husband. Thank the good Lord.

The anesthesiologist came back in within a few minutes. When I told her I was still feeling very intense pain on the right side, she listened and addressed it right away. I was actually prepared to have to go through that whole epidural administration experience again, which I was dreading but not more than the epidural not working on one side during pushing time. But she actually had another big needle/syringe and simply administered it through what was already in place. So, it was really easy, and I was *so* relieved.

Fifteen minutes later, the pain on my right side went away. I was able to rest without pain. Henry didn't have to squeeze my thighs or anything. I could still move my legs. I could still feel the contractions: a strange tightening in my stomach and then I could feel my stomach harden from the outside with my fingers. It was still intense, but no pain.

This is when, after I reassured him five times over, Henry pulled the bed out and slept for two hours.

If I look back, I wish I would have encouraged him to sleep more up to that point. We could have used his energy after the baby was born. Instead, we were both drained by the time our child arrived. Though, thinking now, I'm sure there's no way he would have been able to fall asleep any sooner from everything going on and the excitement of our first baby. He was probably so stressed, anxious, exhilarated . . . So, it's just one of those things that's easier said than done.

An hour or two went by. I'm not sure. I wasn't counting the minutes, only the contractions, only the heart rates. The nurse came in, and I told her that I was feeling pressure on my bum. (From the classes I had taken, I knew that with an epidural, pressure on the bum, as if you might have to poop, was a sign that the baby was approaching.) I told her I was only feeling the pressure during contractions, and she asked me to let her know when I felt it even when I wasn't having a contraction.

More time went by. Henry was still asleep. My night nurse, Grace, asked if I was feeling the pressure beyond contractions, and I said no. She asked if I was ready to check my cervix. I thought about it. I was so exhausted from laboring up to this point, even if I was ready, I didn't feel ready. Plus, I still wasn't feeling that pressure between contractions. So, I asked her if we could wait a little longer. Maybe an hour or so. Then I asked for more water.

While she went to get more water, I thought about it. If I was dilated to ten centimeters, even though I was tired, I was that much closer to meeting the baby. Would an hour really make a difference? Why not just check? I couldn't feel anything. When she brought the water back, I told her that I was okay to check my cervix again.

With her hand up my vagina, she said, "I don't feel anything." This was weird to me because I thought when the cervix was ten centimeters dilated, it was just really open. But the way the nurse described it was as if it had disappeared altogether. She went to get another nurse to confirm that I was fully dilated. This nurse felt around and confirmed. "It's gone."

It was time. I turned and woke Henry up. I had to say his name about ten times before he started to stir, and I felt so bad because he was sleeping so deeply. I told him that we were at ten centimeters. Surprisingly, my fear was gone. I had waited so long. I was ready. *So* ready.

The nurse broke things down for us. She explained how I would be positioned, with my butt out and facing up toward where the wall meets the ceiling. I would hold my thighs up, tilt my head forward, and hold my breath for ten seconds, pushing. I would relax for a second, exhale, inhale, and then hold my breath for ten seconds of pushing. Then I would do it a third time. Three ten-second holds for each contraction and then rest.

I thought about asking to lie on my side. About asking to not hold my breath but breathe through it all. I thought about a lot, but I was tired. This wasn't her first time. So, I slid my butt down and prepared to hold my breath.

She asked Henry if he wanted to hold a leg. He did.

She held the other. While the OB was on her way in, the nurse asked if I wanted to practice. I nodded. So, we did. When I held my breath and pushed for ten seconds, I concentrated all of my "force" or "energy" down to the depths of my abdomen.

The on-call OB came in and explained that my OB was on her way. She asked if I wanted to wait for her to arrive, and I said no. I wanted to push. She then explained everything the nurse did, and she had me try a few pushes with her hands somewhere on me—guiding me where I needed to push. To my relief, she said I was pushing perfectly and to not change a thing. So, I focused on pushing toward my abdomen and not sending the pressure to my head. That became harder as time went by. The more out of breath I became, the more I started pushing up toward my head and running out of breath. My last pushes, I couldn't hold my breath for ten seconds, though I tried.

Now here's the big surprise or reveal. I pushed for two to three hours, starting around midnight. That means I had already been in labor for about fourteen hours (not counting the fact that I had started contractions that morning during the NST). I was tired, but I *loved* the pushing stage. Instead of passively waiting for my cervix to open, I now had a job. I had a breathing pattern, I had to push, and I knew it was the final stage before meeting baby.

I loved the breathing, the holding of breath, the pushing. It felt like back squatting. Like a workout where I was in "the zone." If I had to have guessed (not considering how out of breath and tired I was afterward), I would have thought the pushing stage lasted twenty minutes and not three hours. That's how good it felt.

I kept getting signals to know baby was close. They asked if I wanted to take a break to wait for my own OB again. They said she was fifteen minutes away. I said no. I wanted to keep pushing. I couldn't wait. But that also told me that I might be about fifteen minutes away from meeting baby! More nurses entered the room. There were maybe five surrounding me. They took my right leg that Henry had been holding so he could be up near my head with me. Henry was saying all of the right things, and I heard him, but I don't remember them. He must have known because often between pushing/contractions, he would simply bend down and press his forehead to my forehead, and we closed our eyes together. There just weren't any words left to say.

Dr. Sandy Woods arrived and stood at the center of the circle of nurses. It was funny to see a familiar face. I was going to have the baby with or without her, but it was nice of her to come. I kept pushing. I didn't pause. I was on a mission now.

"Do you want to feel your baby's head?" the on-call OB asked. I said yes. I reached down. I felt the soft wet hair of my baby. My soul, it felt so powerful. Like nothing was going to keep me from that head. I then grabbed my thighs, and I recall saying I was ready to push even if there wasn't a contraction. I could feel the pressure of baby's head where it was. I knew it was there. No pain, just pressure. So close!

They told me it was okay to push without contractions. So, I pushed. Looking back, I should have waited and listened to my body. Instead, I listened to my brain—the most impatient part of me. I wonder if I would have waited for contractions, would I have torn at all?

They started telling me, "Just push for eight seconds."

Then, "Push for five." "One more push to five!" And out the baby came.

I saw the body mass fly up in a blur, and then the baby, purple in color, landed on my belly. I don't remember if I had the belly band around me or not. I think it was gone, and if so, I don't know when it was removed. The monitors were gone. A nurse must have removed them somehow. Oh wait, I remember now. She had cut the band. Everything came off that the band was holding, and the baby was on my body.

But the baby was quiet, and I remember my heart stopping. The nurses and OBs all leapt to the baby with towels, rubbing the baby vigorously. So vigorously that had I not felt so sure that I knew nothing of what was best, I would have told them to stop rubbing my baby like that! I heard someone say my placenta was out. I looked around but could see nothing. It was also then that I admitted to myself that I had no idea what a placenta looked like. I had not felt my placenta leave my body. I still don't understand how I grew an entire organ with my baby, and weirder yet, the baby came out alive and the placenta discarded. It was as if a guardian or protector had brought my baby to me, and I didn't give it so much as a thank you.

I don't remember when Henry said it was a boy. I really don't. I don't remember the moment I found out the gender. But I remember the moment our son began to cry. The moment he made a noise, and I knew he was okay. That, as far as I was concerned, was all that mattered.

My baby—my baby boy—was alive.

11

LETTER TO MY HUSBAND—
PACKED IN OUR HOSPITAL BAGS

Dear Henry,

I don't know when you'll open this letter. I don't know if it's while I'm still in labor and we are waiting, or if it's after the baby comes and somehow you have time to open this. Maybe the worst case has occurred, and this letter is being read when I'm not alive. I'm not trying to be dramatic. I just really don't know.

I thought it would be hard to put all of my feelings into this letter without that context. Without deciding when to tell you to open it or knowing if I'd still be around. But now that I've sat down to write this, it's not hard at all. How I feel about you, about this pregnancy, about the idea of having a baby, of becoming a mother, of you becoming a father, of us remaining strong and devoted to each other, that doesn't change too much.

I know labor will get intense. Medicated or not. But I want you to know that there is no one that comes close to you when I think of who I need by my side as I approach what I know will be the most difficult thing I have ever done. You are my best friend, my husband, but you are so much more, and I'm so glad you're here with me to accompany me through this turbulent process.

When the baby comes, our lives will change. I want you to know that up until the baby comes, I have never loved anyone as much as I love you. And when our baby takes the number one spot, it is only because they represent my closeness and oneness with you. They are the result of this love I have for you and that you have for me that's so far beyond words that writing any such explanation seems a bit pointless. But I want you to know: you have captured my love in a way I could have never guessed, and even though you will hold the number two spot in my heart after our baby, that number two spot will be at a scale that I doubt many can imagine.

If things go wrong with the baby—whatever that may mean—I want you to know that we have each other. That we will get through it. That we will support one another. That we will do what we need and what's best for the baby and their life. That no matter if it's not the life we expected, or if it's not the length we expected, it has already been magical and will continue to be magical in its own unique way—even if it's through a darker lens.

If things go wrong with me—yes, I mean death—I want you to know that I had such an amazing life and that I couldn't picture a happier last six years to close the curtain on. I was given such a lucky life with a healthy body and fun and caring family.

Being able to meet you, to see your face light up when you see the sunrise, and to be treated like an absolute queen by you when, in actuality, I felt I was more potato during the last ten months, I couldn't have been happier. And though I would have, of course, wanted more time with you and our baby, I still am glad we were able to get pregnant and take this journey as far as life allowed.

I only regret that I won't be there to help, but if there are any allowances in the afterlife, or loopholes, or even if I have to break a rule or two, please know I will be there for you in whatever way you need me to be—even if it's you just needing space. And I've said this before: if you have to go on without me, do your best, never keep yourself from happiness, and have so many adventures, and romances, and stories, so that when we meet again, you'll have plenty to share.

Okay, my eyes are swollen and red now writing this, so I want to end it with some positivity.

Whenever you read this, whatever the case, I want you to know what is true. How I feel about you and who you are to me.

You are extremely intelligent. So cunning that you would be a terrifying villain in any story, but the world is lucky in that you are innately good. Mostly, you use your cleverness to be funny in that dark way you have. You have shown me what it means to care for others, including myself, but also your family. You are wildly independent, and you question everything tirelessly. Perhaps this is how you came to be so smart. Your curiosity may be your ultimate superpower.

You're as handsome as you are wholesome. I fell in love with your smile, with your large, rough but careful hands, and the palette of you: olive skin, sandy brown hair, hazel eyes. And the way you smile with your eyes closed when you're pleased by something. There's no better facial expression I have witnessed, and I do as many things as I can to see that look on your face as often as possible. You're strong, hard-working, brave, responsible . . . These might be things that don't cut it on Tinder, but they impress me beyond any surface-level one-liners. You are dependable. You are my rock. You could never let me down, even if you tried.

You are a remarkable person. To know you has been a great gift. To be married to you is some kind of phenomenon in my life I try not to question. To bring someone into this life with you is a miracle that I can only explain by assuming the good karma from a past life has granted me this. No average person would be so lucky.

Thank you for being who you are, for being with me, and for being the father of our child.

I love you with all of my heart.

Evelyn

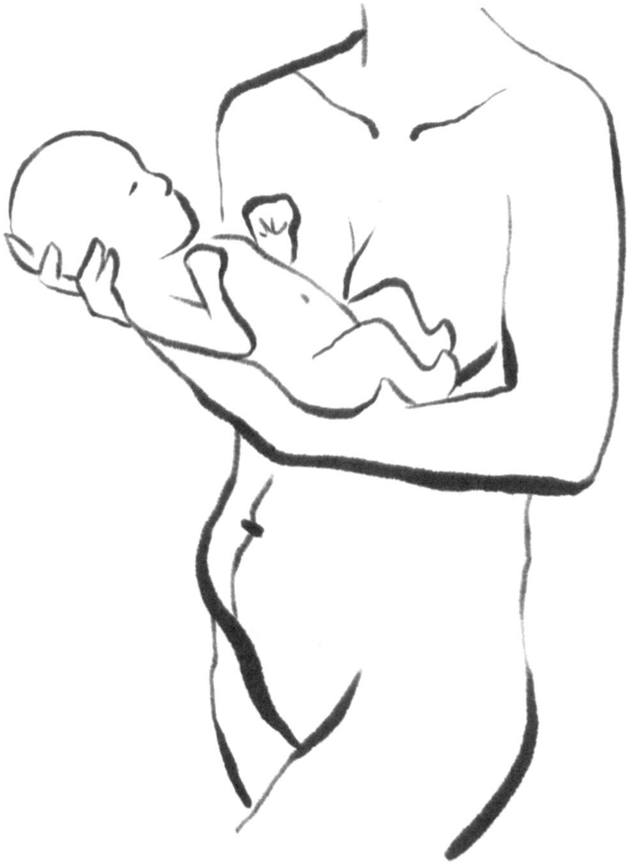

12

THE SUDDEN AWARENESS OF MORTALITY

The first three days of my son's life were the most difficult three days I had ever experienced. The first two weeks of my son's life were the hardest two weeks I had ever experienced, with the first month being the hardest month as well. No baby class I took (*this is how you burp the baby*) and no advice other parents gave me (*Just be kind to yourself*) even came close to preparing me for what was to come.

After labor and delivery, my body was wheeled out by a nurse while I held the soft, damp infant in my arms. My husband wheeled our bags, pillows, and car seat beside me. When I had first been offered a wheelchair when I arrived at the hospital, I had turned down the offer, thinking it was silly because I was so . . . able to walk. When I sat in the wheelchair, being rolled from labor and delivery to the recovery room, I found the idea of walking quite impossible. After seventeen hours of labor and a second-degree tear somewhere in the dark gaping hole between my legs, I had made it to the "recovery" room, where it felt like I did everything but recover.

I was transferred from the wheelchair to the bed. My husband put the cargo down in the corner. He walked to the corner of the room, where a nurse showed him how to swaddle the baby for the first time. From the bed, I strained to see the rest of my family. I could see my baby's legs and the serious look my husband had on his face as he watched the first of many blanket wrappings our son would be conquered—or not conquered—by.

There were many women in the room surrounding my husband and my baby. It was bright, and then it was dark. Without being able to piece it together through bright, lively, swift chatter, my husband and I were somehow left alone in the dark room with our baby. Our son was in a small, plastic-looking hospital bed on wheels next to me. My husband on the pull-out sofa.

The catheter was still attached to me, so I didn't need to use the restroom just yet. The IV was still attached as well. When would these things be removed? I wanted them out.

It was quiet. So unbelievably quiet. And yet so simply unbelievable I took a deep inhale to launch into my first sob for a much-needed meltdown—when I was interrupted. My vent session stalled.

A small cry cut through the silence, through the darkness, through the sob forming in my throat. My child. My newborn's cry. How can I explain how it sounded? Like I had taken this soul from its peaceful place and wretched it out into a world full of cold and hot and loud and bright. To a place where hunger was relentless, and yet nutrition must be consumed from another body with a new, difficult, and exerting act rather than how it was before: continuously flowing from one body to its own, effortlessly. It was the sound of a being that knew I had taken him from that safe, warm, easy harbor and wanted me to know that for the rest of my life, I would pay for it.

From this realization, the baby let out this anguish. I felt bewildered, but before I had the time to cry angrily in response (for this little tyke was stealing my terrible and great thunder), I realized the strength of the cry was still . . . small. The breath was short. The cry only contained the beginnings and endings of shrieks with no middle tone. The baby was too small, too young to let out the long, bellowing wails he desired. He was too fragile, and I knew he couldn't communicate all of the pains he wanted to tell me about. So, he chose one pain to communicate—a pain a deeper part of me, a primal part, could not ignore: hunger.

My pain, my anguish, my fear, it all disappeared. I rushed to my baby. I only needed to turn and prop myself up, to lift my baby from his box to my own hospital bed. But it took more effort and coordination than I had anticipated. The process just to bring him to my breast was enough to prompt the trembling of my body. It didn't matter, though, not once he latched onto my nipple. Whenever he did and began sucking, I thanked God I didn't have any latching issues that I had heard others had. I sat in the darkness, tears sliding down my cheeks for the mothers who could not respond to the hunger cry in the way they had hoped.

I had often heard mothers say, "I bore you into this world." I always shrunk back from that kind of mentality. The mentality that children owed their mothers for bringing them into the world. I was told that once I had a child, I would understand the sentiment. Now on the other side, I'm relieved to know my resentment of that ideology has not gone away. Instead, I now understand why I disagreed. It was common sense: all mothers owed their children for bringing them into this world.

That is why when they're cold, we warm them. Why when they're wet, we change them. Why when they're hungry, we feed them. And we do those things until death, when we return to wherever we go before and after life, where we will leave this world of constant bodily needs and our children will eventually join us and confront us with a smug and simple: *if the world was so great, why did you come back here?*

In the recovery room, I was unable to sleep for more than a few minutes at a time. I was woken up to take medication, to sign medical papers, to submit a birth certificate, to learn how to breastfeed, to be asked about my pain, to be helped to the toilet, to be detached from my catheter, from my IV, to order food, to be given food, to permit my son to be tested for hearing and sight, to vaccinate my child, to do more things than should have been possible in the forty-eight hours or so we were there.

I remember my son being rolled away for the hearing and vision test. The nurse said he would be gone for fifteen to thirty minutes. I realized this would be fifteen to thirty minutes where I would not be disturbed. Where no cry of hunger could send me into action. I agreed with the hope of sleep in mind, and as soon as the door shut and my baby was no longer in the room, I wondered about him. I worried about him. I obsessed over the absence of him from our room as well as the existence of him elsewhere.

What if they got mixed up and returned the wrong

baby? What if he was deaf, or blind, or both? What if they found something else wrong with the test? What if they were too rough with him? What if he was crying and needed me and I was in here sleeping? What if—

Before I could think of another scenario, he was returned to me. Hungry. I welcomed him, completely and utterly sleep-deprived and exhausted. But he was safe, and that was the only thing that I could process. No sleep or rest could defeat my demons now. Only his safety.

When we left the hospital, still under the seventy-two-hour mark, I recall watching one of the nurses show us how to fit our son into his brand-new car seat. I nodded, watching carefully and taking in her instruction. However, I looked at my son. Examined him. Closed eyes, red-pigmented face, no neck, tiny fists, soft, fleshy skin. He would not survive a car accident. There was just no way a human this small with all of the fancy straps in the world could survive it. I doubted he could survive much at this point. He was so small, so delicate. It was then a line came to me I had read once: "His mortality was always with me, constant as a second beating heart." I couldn't recall then where it was from. But I related to these words too much, and they haunted me as we clicked him into the car seat base in our SUV.

I was relieved to find my husband believed the same. We did not speak when he drove, but I knew he felt the same because he drove five under the speed limit and we avoided the highway. This was very unlike Henry, and as if worrying about a small baby wasn't enough, it was then that I realized I was desperate for Henry to continue living as well. It wasn't just my baby I would worry about. As capable as I thought I once was, I could not raise Oliver on my own. My eyes scattered as we approached each intersection. I was ready to holler at the sign of any impending danger. *Please, God*, I thought. *If one of us must die, make it me. I cannot bear the idea of my son or husband's death. Henry is stronger than me. Let them live and take me instead.*

There was no accident. No member of the family was called by the reaper. It was somehow unbelievable to me that all three of us had been spared and made it safely home.

When we pulled up to our house, I recall how I felt. My eyes were so tired, they were dry, causing me to constantly blink. My lips cracked and flaky. My tailbone throbbed. My labia burned. My spine tingled on the inside and itched on the outside. I took slow, careful steps and used both rails when taking the five stairs up to our front door. My husband carried our son. The welcome mat lay in front of us. We looked at each other for a moment, each of us realizing our home would never be how we had left it again. That we were beginning a new era. I unlocked the door and opened it. My husband waited until our eyes locked before he took his first step inside our house. The first time in our house as parents.

The next twenty-four hours would continue to be part of the hardest three days of my life. There was no sleep. There was no strength. There was no escape. Survival, I had accepted, was impossible. I was simply waiting for my body and soul to fade away and dissolve into nothing as I continued to try to function and run on no sleep, no nutrition, and—most obvious—no experience.

There were peaceful moments, but even in the most peaceful moments, when Oliver suckled from my breast, eyes closed, hands slowly loosening from a demanding fist to a content open palm, I still worried something might go wrong. I could not smile, and I could not laugh without wondering if Henry or Oliver would unexpectedly, for lack of a better phrase, drop dead.

The only time I wasn't worrying was when another irritant had superseded my anxiety. It might have been screams from Oliver, our baby's unwillingness to negotiate sleeping without our touch, or visitors trying to push their way through the door to give baby a kiss. It was all a type of stress. The adoring smiles, the baby coos, the little moments of joy I had been promised by every diaper commercial I had come across. *Where were they?* I wondered. They weren't to be found. How old were the babies who were on the Gerber baby ads? When did my baby start to look like that? When would my baby be able to track me with their eyes? Know me with their fingers? Smile by my voice?

When?

No. I think back. No class. No advice. Nothing prepared me for this. No one painted the picture of the ordeal we had faced. I only felt this incredible sense of worry. A new weight on my heart of dread as I checked to make sure my sleeping baby was still breathing. I wrestled with an ungodly lack of sleep i would never catch up on. The bathing, the feeding, the bouncing and swaying, the diaper changing... I could not keep up. And through what I still undoubtedly recall as a unique type of suffering—a suffering that was born from love—a thought instantly teased my mind: This wasn't just the life I chose, this was the life I deserved.

13

RANDOM THOUGHT OF A MOTHER #1

Where: Driving to the grocery store.

When: Two in the afternoon when Oliver and Henry are both napping.

What: Oliver is Henry's middle name. Why do I have no desire to give one of my names to our future children if we have a daughter? Is that just a guy thing? You hear about Fred Jr., but you never hear about Jessica Jr.

14

PHANTOM CRIES

There is a thing that you might Google like I once Googled. This is the one thing you might not talk to your doctor about because you're afraid you are losing your mind. You're literally afraid they'll tell you you're losing it. Here's what you might Google:

Why do I hear my baby crying when he's not actually crying?

After the search, you will learn what phantom cries are. Then you will not worry if you are losing your mind or if you are the only one that hears these cries. But you will wonder—hearing cries in the night that don't exist, a belly that swells and shrinks like the tides, a heart that drips sustenance through the chest for another being—what else will motherhood bring?

15

THE OTHERS

Though I didn't want any visitors at the hospital, keeping family at bay wasn't an issue on my side of the family. During the week of my due date, Cosmic had already put a deposit down for a sex retreat in Mexico. Angelica had already purchased tickets for Coachella for the entire week. And my youngest sister, Mia, you may recall, decided to go on an impromptu road trip to Disneyland with her college boyfriend the day I went into labor. My mother, who said she would be there if I needed her, was unfortunately unvaccinated on all fronts and refused to wear a mask in the hospital. So, not only was she not welcome to visit our baby without her shots so soon after the baby was born but she wasn't allowed to enter the hospital because masks infringed upon her rights.

On Henry's side, it was somewhat of the opposite. All members had all of the vaccines recommended for adults who were to be around children, and those who didn't had gotten updated shots well before our due date to make sure they could be holding hands with our baby while he was still making his way out of my body (if we would have let them).

Henry's family dropped off food and groceries the first week and saw the baby from afar by day three. I was thankful for Henry's family, who often offered food or help with the chores. By the first week, though it was not part of the plan, almost all of his family had held Oliver in their arms. I thought we might protest a bit longer, but when they asked, Henry only looked at me sheepishly as if I were the parent who had been asked if they could open a Christmas present before it was Christmas. I obliged.

My family finally made Oliver's acquaintance when he was two months old. They did not offer to come to us, and instead, we drove to grandma's five hours away. I'll never forget the feeling of walking in. Angelica approached quickly. She took Oliver from me without even looking at me. No greeting. I remember the feeling of transferring his weight into her hands as I thought, *You never called me. Not even once these past ten months. Not when I needed you most.* She held him in her arms. I was hesitant to let go. Then she took her phone out of her pocket. I watched her take seventy-three selfies with him in her arms before she handed him back to me. She still had not acknowledged me or Henry. Only my child and her own phone. I squeezed Oliver tightly and looked to Henry, who was giving me sideways glances to make sure I was okay.

Angelica turned her phone to me and showed me a filtered image of her and my son already posted onto Instagram with the caption, "Proud aunt! Couldn't wait to meet this little guy!" I looked at her. *You waited two months to meet him.* Before I could open my mouth, she turned away, plopped on the couch, and began to scroll to refresh her Instagram notifications. It had been painful but quick. It was over.

Next, Cosmic approached slowly. She tilted her head, looking at Oliver.

"He is cute," she decided.

"Thank you."

"Can I hold him?" she asked.

"Of course." I handed Oliver off more willingly this time.

I watched Cosmic hold him. Every movement was slow and intentional. She looked into Oliver's eyes for any signals. Mia had leaned over to look closely at my son's face from over the shoulder of our eldest sister. Mia was curious but still too afraid yet to hold him. Though, after seeing Cosmic manage to rock my baby with ease, Mia finally took her turn.

I thought about how I had let Angelica snatch Oliver away from me. How my anger and my thoughts were bottled up inside. I wanted to be the mother who could stand firm, who could communicate her emotions eloquently. I wanted to point out that Angelica hadn't even greeted me or my husband. I wanted to tell all of my sisters that I was hurt when they never reached out—and somehow do it with polite authority so I could make a point, feel heard, but not make it an argument. But I knew I couldn't.

I wasn't the mother I had hoped to be yet. Instead, I had given Oliver up to avoid conflict instead of keeping him like my heart so desperately wanted to do. I watched Oliver get passed around in short spurts with a strange ache in my heart. It was a pain that came from knowing I wasn't holding my baby when I cared the most about him. It was the sensation of attempting to share someone precious with people I loved who would never possibly understand his value. It was missing someone before he had even left my fingertips.

My mother held him the most, though her focus was not on my son but on her past as a mother. While letting him burrow in her arms, she would recount the mistakes she made and demand I do better. *I never took care of myself after the baby was born and let myself go. I neglected my marriage and lost my husband. Not once after I became pregnant did I put on a nice outfit, so I never felt good about myself. I only focused on my children and never had my own career.*

It was exhausting and depressing to hear my mother's regrets in the disguise of advice. She was relentless with her warnings in between babytalk with my son. Though she seemed happy now, of all the things she told me she wished she would have done differently, I began to wonder if really the one thing she would have changed was having any children at all.

After four days, my milk supply had dropped to barely being able to keep Oliver full. My spirits were low. My family had slept in late and wanted to spend more time together in the evening hours when it was time to put Oliver down. My mother had moved us to a bedroom farther away so that the cries of our child wouldn't wake them in the mornings or during their naps or disrupt them while they watched movies. The window of time we all had together was actually quite small. This is where Cosmic would try to match Oliver's energy, which she described as peaceful. When Angelica would get more likes on Instagram before I had posted a single photo of him on my own account. Mia would ask questions about what he ate or how much he slept. Her polite interest was rather easy to match, and our conversations felt the most normal. My mother started to ask about my work and wondered how we would manage with Henry as the primary caretaker.

Henry, who had encouraged me to leave our guest bedroom and mingle with my family, had been satisfied with the quality time spent at grandma's after three days. By that time, my yearning for the attention of my mother and siblings turned sour. I couldn't tell if my irritation was stemming from the fact that nobody had reached out to me while I was pregnant or the fact that I hoped they didn't reach out for just as long after we left. By the fifth day, I told Henry it was time to go home. I needed distance between me and my family. I wanted Oliver back in my arms without being obligated to share, and it was at the end of the trip that I had also admitted that a lot of the tension was brewing from my unwillingness to separate with my baby and less to do with the people I was sharing Oliver with. There was more I needed to work through on my own, but I couldn't do it at my mother's house.

On the drive home, Henry, Oliver, and I were completely drained. We were so tired that it took us a week to unpack. I met with a lactation consultant to come up with a pumping strategy to increase my milk supply that was still long in drought. (The hardest part was trying not to worry about my milk supply being low because worrying only decreased my milk supply.) But we decompressed slowly back at home. We fell into the familiar safety of continuous loads of laundry and endless diaper changes that soon occupied our minds, replacing the strange anxieties that came from family visits. My milk supply returned a week later, and I finally started to feel calm again.

What had happened during that trip was getting the confirmation that my sisters and my mother were not going to be close with me (and I with them) in the way that we were before. There had been no misunderstanding that my siblings wanted to clear up about them not calling when I was pregnant or for waiting so long to meet Oliver. I personally didn't mind having to wait, but I admit I was envious of Henry's family, who fought over who would hold Oliver next. My sisters simply didn't care, and perhaps my mother cared too much but couldn't deliver the support I needed while postpartum.

I would have mourned those relationships, but I was too relieved to not have to put in my monthly calls anymore. It made me wonder if my once-a-month obligatory calls to my sisters were actually worse than their approach of inaction. All that would happen now was that I would stop calling them once a month, and our relationships would grow stale but not unpleasant—from a distance.

I was different now, and everything was different along with me.

It was true. I had been pregnant (twice); I had had a baby; I had become a mother and Henry a father. I was "the Other." The isolation, the loneliness, the feeling of falling back into the shadows. It was real, and it was a consolation to my tired body.

I had a few childless friends who lived out of state that called to check on me, called to congratulate me, and I was grateful for their calls. But it wasn't the same. Just like their lives had felt distant when I was pregnant, our lives now felt like they were being played out in different dimensions. I still enjoyed our talks, but they were short and, if I dare say, lacking any depth. I include myself in that statement. I just couldn't get invested while having nothing to offer up other than thoughts on Oliver's ever-evolving sleeping schedule.

But then, something happened.

One day, I was scrolling through Instagram when I saw an image of Oliver I had taken and sent to my sisters and mother in our group text thread posted on Instagram. Angelica had posted the photo on her Instagram minutes later. She hadn't tagged me in the photo. She hadn't mentioned me in any way, shape, or form. (Why would she? She didn't even say hello to me when we drove five hours to visit.) I was annoyed.

Henry and I had agreed social media was OK as long as the images were appropriate. In that moment, I wished we had been against it. However, I felt like avoiding social media was a losing battle with my children—just as it was then with Angelica. I still hadn't posted anything, and Oliver was still out there on the internet. Not just on Angelica's account but on my mother-in-law's Facebook and my sister-in-law's TikTok. It was inevitable.

But then I decided, well I should get to post a photo too. So, I did. I finally welcomed Oliver into the world. I wrote a few things about him being born, a light joke about becoming a mother, a shout-out to Henry.

Many likes came in. Lots of comments were left. I hadn't been sure about sharing this all on social media, but it was nice to get the acknowledgment. It felt petty. It felt adolescent. The joy I got from reading, "Congratulations," and, "He is so perfect," over and over again. I started to resent myself. I started to regret sharing my child.

Then something else happened. I got private messages.

Friends that I had all but abandoned when they became pregnant reached out, offering to be a shoulder or ear when I needed to cry or vent. Old classmates from college, now also working moms, took screenshots of pages from a book on sleep training that had been "life-changing." Coworkers from past and current jobs were ready to talk about pumping schedules and ask me about my body and recovery. A stranger who I had become friends with over our interest in reading romance novels had had her first baby days apart from Oliver, and we both wrote long messages back and forth in the wee hours of the morning while breastfeeding and pumping. We had no advice to share but only humble, frightening confessions about being a mother. They checked in when there were formula and infant Tylenol shortages to let me know they had some if I was in need.

I had found my people. Or, more accurately, my people had found me.

Within a week, I was out on stroller walks with previous coworkers. A sound machine that was a favorite of a friend's kids had been delivered to us, and dinner was dropped off on my porch by an old friend who now had two children. (I had let our relationship evaporate when her first child was born).

I had brunch with a friend, another mother of two, and she talked about postpartum depression. She had exercised, she had eaten nutritious meals, but it wasn't until she started taking medication that she was able to level out and, in her words, save her marriage. I talked to her about how much I hated letting Oliver go and having others hold him. I was able to confide in her about the hours I spent just watching him sleep to make sure his little chest was moving the way it was designed to. We laughed about how much hemorrhoids made us cry.

In a single Instagram post, I found women and men who related to me, understood me, who laughed and cried with me without feeling ashamed or having to apologize. Before, I had accepted myself as the Other. I had figured I didn't deserve to revive friendships I had let die when my friends had become pregnant, but they had reached out to me without judgment or grudges. For the first time since I had become pregnant, I felt I wasn't alone.

16

POSTPARTUM APPOINTMENT CHECKLIST (IN ORDER OF IMPORTANCE)

Twenty four questions you may ask:
1. When can I take full baths, and when can I get deep tissue massages?
2. How long should I wait before having sex again?
3. Is it OK to start exercising again? Is anything off-limits?
4. Are there foods I shouldn't eat while breastfeeding?
5. Are any medications off-limits?
6. What can I do about my postpartum discomforts/pains (oh-my-god-the-hemorrhoids, backaches, sore breasts, sensitive nipples, etc.)?
7. I can still feel pain in the area where the epidural was inserted. Is that normal, and when will it go away?
8. Does my emotional state seem normal to you?
9. How is my healing going down there, and do I need to see a pelvic floor specialist or physical therapist?
10. My breasts. What pain is normal? What isn't?
    a. I have pain for the first three to five seconds when latching, and then it goes away. It feels like my nipple is getting pierced by a needle. It almost feels good because

mentally I know relief is coming when the baby is starting to empty me out.

b. My breasts are really sore throughout the day. Things like running would be very uncomfortable. Can I manage this better?

c. Some areas when I press on my breasts hurt very badly. Almost as if I'm pressing on a burn or deep bruise. Can I manage this better? Is this a sign of infection?

11. How do I know if I have a blocked duct? I've read about blocked ducts. I really, really don't want to get one.

12. I have some marks on the bottom side of my breasts that are red/purple. If these are stretch marks, I'm not worried. I'm worried about mastitis or something developing and want to make sure I'm being proactive. I've seen photos of mastitis on the internet. I really, really don't want to get mastitis.

13. What is the ideal routine for me and pumping and breastfeeding, especially during the night? Right now, my breasts get so full that I am having to pump/feed every two to three hours, and it's closer to two hours, even through the night.

14. How long can I sleep at night, though uncomfortable, without decreasing my milk supply?

15. After I finish nursing my baby, my breasts are still quite full unless I pump afterward. I'm worried that he's not getting enough. How can I be sure? Also, will I ever feel fully empty?

16. For heat and massage for my breasts, how exactly do I do that?

a. How do I massage my breasts when feeding my baby? Like, how do I massage myself while holding an infant at the same time?

b. How do I put heat around my breasts when feeding without burning my baby?

c. What do these things—heating, massaging, cooling — physically look like? What position is the baby in? How do I hold myself and the baby? Can you show me?

17. I use my vibrator to massage my breasts. Is that weird?

18. How do I breastfeed without my hands, forearms, fingers getting tired/cramping from holding my baby? My limbs feel like they're going to fall off my shoulders.

19. What is the recommended amount of breastmilk I should freeze "just in case"?

20. Hands-free pump. Is it worth it? I have a Spectra, but I don't get a lot of milk unless I'm putting pressure on my boob with my other hand (expressing), so I can't really do anything else anyway (or even pump both at once for that matter).

21. Is it normal to not pump a lot of milk the first five to ten minutes of a session?

22. Tell me more about "letdown." I think I know what it is, but I'm not sure.

23. When should I stop breastfeeding?

24. When can we have another baby?

17

RANDOM THOUGHT OF A MOTHER #2

Where: In the bath.

When: Approximately 8:45 a.m., while Oliver is crying during naptime, but I have agreed not to disturb him until 9:30 a.m.

What: To think that some couples have children to "save the marriage." It's laughable. It's a selfish act that one does only out of denial. Please, if your marriage is struggling and you don't have a healthy way to strengthen it but no courage to break it off, have an affair with a man who has no children. At least that way you won't be including a young, innocent life as part of the collateral damage.

18

BATHTIME

Massages and baths. There was sex, there was exercise, there was swimming. My first question in my postpartum checkup was, "Am I healthy and healed enough for massages and baths?"

After getting the greenlight to do all of the above, I came home and immediately started my first period since becoming pregnant. Six weeks after the baby came exactly. The first day, I wasn't sure if it actually was my period. After the blood showed, I scheduled a massage for the soonest available, which was in two weeks' time. Then, the second day after being cleared for the water and continuing to bleed the familiar textures of tangled string and goop, I said fuck it and drew a bath.

The only bath in our house was upstairs in what used to be a crawl space of an attic. My husband had turned it into my workspace when Covid hit, and with an awkward corner leftover, I begged him for a bathtub. He had immediately gone to work. The tub was now part of an open loft with no door separating it from my office or even the downstairs. My work had contaminated my self-care routine long ago anyway—no matter how strongly I denied it. Without being able to wait for the tub to fill, I lay inside it as I turned the faucet on in excitement. My first bath since the baby.

Once the temperature was adjusted, I leaned back and felt the sting of the cool porcelain on my back. I could hear our son trying to decide if he was content or upset between the words my husband was speaking to him in a falsetto, singsong voice he had adopted once the baby arrived. It pained me that my husband had to sacrifice his time and patience for me to gain some time and patience upstairs. The fact that I couldn't completely relax and ignore the cries or coos of my child and make the most of his sacrifice only added salt to the wound. But lying there, I knew I'd never be able to completely relax when my child was alive because that—my child alive—meant that there was the possibility that my child could be hungry, could be scared, could get hurt, could die, and there was no bathtub setup that could convince me otherwise.

Even under the care of the person I loved and trusted most, I worried for my son in a way that made even the idea of something getting into his eye and watering his vision for only a few moments unacceptable. The guilt that I mentioned before came because any time or luxury I took for myself meant my husband had to cover for me. My small joys would only be had if he gave up one of his.

I turned off the water and lay still. A few small bubbles the size of baby ladybugs sprung to the surface of the water just near my pubic bone. A queef. I had probably queefed twice my whole life—and only after some very intense sex—before becoming pregnant. Now my lower cavity had a mind of its own and free will at that. It was clear that I wasn't aware of the control I had lost over my body since my first trimester began. It wasn't something I could feel, but there would be moments like this where visuals would be my cue. It was the extra skin surrounding my belly button I would see jiggling when my baby sat on top of my abdomen at night before I burped him. It was the bareness of my scalp in several different spots on my once thick-maned head. And this afternoon, it was the sprawling bubbles that appeared during my sacred and solo bathtime.

My Instagram feed had conveyed to me that a lot of these visual cues caused distress among us mothers. Sometimes because they said so, but other times because their captions said their changes were okay and that it should be normalized.

I often read these captions and feel nothing. I know I am not a champion of women. I know I am not a significant part of the mother community online or in person. I see these images of puffy stomachs, stretch marks, dark linea nigras, and the call to normalize these things, and I just don't feel the way I know these women want me to feel. I don't think, "You are strong, Jessica. Thank you for showing me your belly button." I don't think, "Yes, let's stop showing skinnier mothers who recover like Barbie dolls." I only think, "When have our bodies ever felt normal, and why must we call on others to make it so?"

I understand it helps with shame, and guilt, and body image, and that is why I don't respond with my thoughts. I hope each pocket of the world can normalize what they'd like to see more of, but really, truly, I just want to take a fucking bath.

So, I put my phone away, because I'm not the hero other mommies need, and I picked up a book. The cover was blue and the size of the author's name was so similar to the size of the book title that no matter how long I stared at the cover, I couldn't tell which was bigger. The reminder kicks me—almost reminding me of when I had a little body inside of me that would nudge me every now and then—*I want to write a book.*

I opened the book to the bookmarked page, a page I had read last before the baby had come. The reminder again, but stronger. *I need to write a book.* I started on the fourth chapter and cruised through a handful of pages. Then I read a line that was written with such style that I read it a second and third time. The reminder screamed in my ear: *I must become published. I must have a book cover. Green! And my name must be printed the same size as my book title if not larger. And I want it in physical form so readers can accidentally drop it into the water while they take a bath!*

I continued reading with all of my body submerged in the water except my head, neck, and knees. Only two minutes passed when I felt a stinging alarm from my breasts with an intensity piercing both of my nipples. The pain was so sudden that my eyes left a sentence before I had reached the end and looked down at my chest.

At first, I was under the impression that my areolas were on fire. White, smoky strands floated from each nipple, clouding the water over my breast and collarbone. It took me a moment to realize that I had not caught fire while underwater like some witch and was actually experiencing my motherly, milky letdown. (*But I had just pumped!*)

That's when I lowered my book because I thought I felt another spurt of bubbles leave my body from below. I peeked over the top of the page expecting to see the result of another queef. I didn't see bubbles. Instead, I saw ribbons of orange, red, and brown. My blood. But I still wasn't sure if it was residual blood from the trauma of birth or if it was blood from the potential of the unthinkable: becoming pregnant once again. Postpartum blood or period blood—and really did it matter?

I reluctantly closed my book. I set it down on the table. I left the escape my book was giving me. But only to be present in this tub of what was filled with the ingredients of life, of death, of sustenance. It was bitter, sweet, warm, thick. If I had been some goddess, I might have been able to see the beginning of my life all the way to the end in the enchanted and swirling red-and-white ripples. The liquid I lay in was entirely magical and disgusting all at the same time. It seemed that motherhood was full of juxtapositions like that in small and spectacular ways. The best and worst. The easiest and hardest. The beginning and end. All brought together in this pool of water.

For a few more moments, I stared at the water—what was underneath the surface and what had risen to the top. My vagina had only bled more, and the water was a muddy red between my legs. It was as if my upper body was smoking as a result of the lower half of my body being on fire. It was the true reminder: *I am a mother now. Forever. Always.*

I looked down at myself and took a snapshot in my head. I imagined adding a filter to my naked body and its literal water-coloring abilities and posting the photo of my naked, submerged, postpartum body on Instagram for all to see with the caption:

"Can we please normalize milk and blood?"

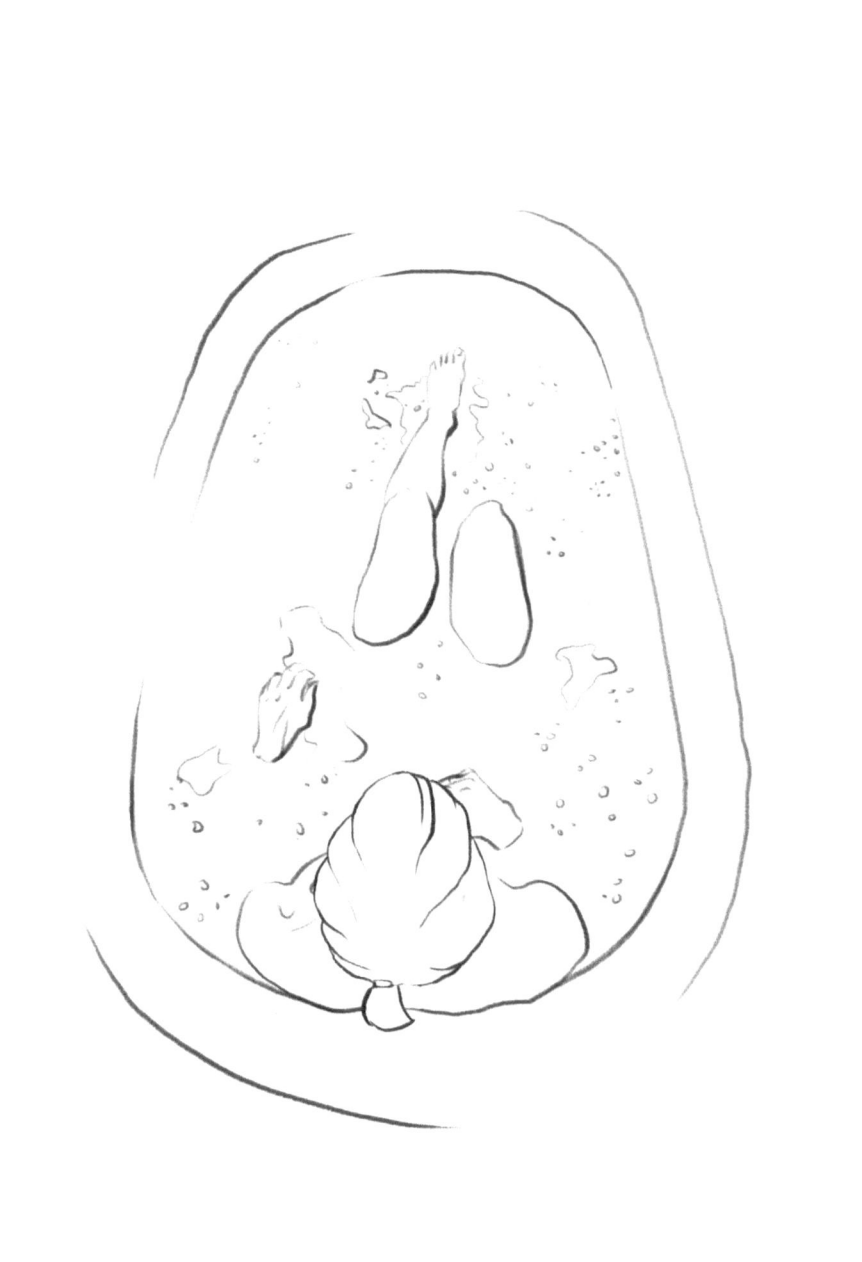

19

CARELESS WHISPER FIGHTS

Henry and I are very different on the surface. I'm an extrovert. He's an introvert. I like farmers' markets. He likes when I bring him home something from the farmers' market. On the inside, we're very similar. I didn't realize how much we think alike until we had been dating for a very long time. We think very similarly; we feel very different.

But opposites attract. No?

Our similarities and differences are both strengths and weaknesses in our relationship. When Oliver came, those strengths and weaknesses were amplified. From our strengths, we are a reliable team. We do more so the other can do less. I happily take the early shifts so Henry can sleep. Henry changes as many diapers as humanly possible so I can focus on breastfeeding and have more rest time in between. I make a list, and Henry gets the groceries. I watch Oliver so Henry can de-stress with a favorite video game, and he takes over when I need to unwind in the bathtub. This came naturally to us.

Oliver's existence brought our weaknesses into the spotlight immediately as well.

After seventeen hours of labor and the anxiety that comes from not wanting the life we created to die, we started our lives as a family completely and utterly sleep-deprived. In the wee hours of the morning, you might have caught Henry and I standing over the crib, whisper-fighting over which way the Binky should go in.

"It's upside down," I hissed. I'm shirtless, and my milky breasts bounce with my quiet exclamation.

"There is no upside or downside. It's just a Binky," Henry replied. His hair is wild in the middle of the night, and without his glasses, he's squinting in the dark.

"The nipple is lopsided now, and it'll wake him up. He won't sleep as long," I counter.

"It literally doesn't matter."

"If it doesn't matter, why don't you just put the Binky in right side up, so it doesn't bother me?"

"Do what you want."

"I do what I want—the problem is that you don't do what I want."

All the while, Oliver was fast asleep. By the time we would realize we were arguing about nothing, Oliver would wake up, and our anger mixed with a little bit of disbelief and exhaustion would spill over into the following morning, though neither of us were quite aware of how dominant its presence was.

At breakfast, we found friction again. Henry didn't look up when he entered the kitchen. There was no "good morning" anymore, and the least I felt he could do was to acknowledge me after I took care of the 4:00 a.m. disturbance coming from Oliver's crib.

"Are you okay?" I asked.

"I'm fine, Evelyn."

"You only use my name when you're mad."

"I'm not mad. I'm just frustrated."

"Semantics."

"Okay. Whatever . . . Evelyn."

He knew I hated it when he used my name like that. I recall that morning wishing so badly that Henry didn't know my name. It gave him too much power. It made me too angry. I closed my eyes and clenched my jaw. Then he poured me a cup of coffee and asked me to pass the creamer. I obliged. Damn. Folgers tasted good on no sleep.

As angry as we got, as stupid as the fights became, we needed each other more than ever. Raising a baby somehow had us at each other's throats, but deep down we knew that if we weren't able to do it together, there was no way we could do it alone. With apologies and forgiveness, and oftentimes without apologies and forgiveness, we poured the coffee and passed the creamer.

The fights were different from fights before the baby. They were about less important things—seemingly. They went from zero to one hundred, fast. I needed more control when I felt I didn't have any as a parent, and Henry needed more freedom when he, too, lost that when Oliver was born. The balance we had created as a childless couple was off. There was only chaos, and every argument, though stupid and only loud in size, but not in importance, added up. I had crying fits where I ran upstairs and threw myself on a pile of pillows where I had used to read for hours on end before the baby came. Henry withdrew downstairs into his den where he used to have video game marathons, and now he would sit in silence and stew.

My hormones were turning me back into a teenager.

Henry was having to deal with that teenager. We both weren't getting any sleep, and when an argument started over "nothing," the more ridiculous the cause of the fight, the angrier we seemed to get.

Granted, there were real things happening. I couldn't let go of Oliver completely. I was so careful with my baby, and I wanted everyone—including my husband—to mirror my behavior with my son. Henry envied the bonds of pregnancy and breastfeeding that he could never have. He was frustrated with only a bottle a day to connect with Oliver in that way, and I rarely gave him more than a bottle because pumping was so time-consuming and made my nipples much sorer than feeding Oliver directly from my chest.

We admitted to this when we were calm. But when we were angry, all of our frustration was focused on how the hell did all of Oliver's matching socks disappear? Where did all of the burping towels go? Why did Henry have to shut doors so loudly? And why did I watch Henry without blinking when he bottle-fed our baby?

More often than not, we never found the answer to these questions. Especially in the heat of the moment. Even after the heat of the moment, I dreaded what little thing would set us both off next. It was hard not knowing what would end up causing an argument with us stomping off—whoever had Oliver taking him with them. My only consolation was that Oliver could not understand our swears or pettiness. My fear was that Henry and I wouldn't get our shit together before he did start to piece together our arguments and understand what our huffing and puffing was all about.

20

THE MILK MEMO

Now, I offer a disclaimer here to say that I didn't choose to breastfeed Oliver because it's magical. It's not. Most of the time it's messy. It can be painful. It's inconvenient. It's exhausting. No. Magical isn't the first word that comes to mind. I talked to my pediatrician, and we reviewed the pros and cons. We talked about the benefits of breastfeeding and sized those benefits up against the drawbacks. I chose to breastfeed because I wanted myself and my child to get the benefits of breastfeeding. I did so also knowing I would be cheerfully flexible if breastfeeding ever became detrimental to me or my baby, be it emotionally, mentally, or physically. And I have already veered off that path. The first week of Oliver's life, he lost more than 10 percent of his body weight and had jaundice. We immediately supplemented with formula until my milk supply came in and stabilized. I didn't hesitate for a moment to change up my strategy to ensure my baby was getting what he needed. When things improved and my milk came in, I changed my strategy again. I will continue to breastfeed and have goals in mind, but I'm flexible and Henry is supportive of whatever I choose. This was best—for me. What's best for you and your baby? You tell me. Or don't. Your call.

Now, let's continue.

Here's a day in the life of breastfeeding starting at 5:55 a.m. This is when Oliver begins to stir. His eyes open, and he moves his head side to side in that cute way that pulls the hair out from the back of his head and gives him the signature bald spot that most babies showcase in their crib days. I sometimes wait for a small whimper or cry before I get up to take him from the crib and bring him back to the bed where I feed him, but this time my breasts were huge, hard, engorged, and leaking. I needed him to nurse more than he needed me to nurse at that point.

I first pick him up to change a heavy, wet diaper. He smiles when he sees me, dipping his little chin into his nonexistent neck. I whisper, "Good morning," and then pick him up. Oliver stares at me as I take him to the changing table. My coordination is never great in the morning, but I somehow manage to attach the soft bands around his waist over a dry diaper. Then I take him to bed.

In my arms, his weight is reassuring. His warmth, loving. His eyes are not yet fully open, but his mouth is open to full capacity. With a gaping, searching mouth, his head swivels left and right until I insert the whole of my nipple into his mouth. I feel his tongue first. Then I feel his lips close around my areola, and the sucking begins with a piercing pain as if there was a needle being inserted into my nipple to begin the milk transfer. After five to seven seconds, the sharp pain fades away, and Oliver's milk-removing skills feel so good on my chest that I let out a deep sigh. Henry hears my relief and squeezes my hand or holds Oliver's foot or taps his little toes before rolling over to catch up on the sleep he gave up for the late-night shift.

If Oliver isn't hungry enough, he might not empty my breasts as much as I need to feel full relief before starting the day. That would mean I would have to pump directly after this. Sometimes I pump after he eats a lot just to keep my milk supply up for pumping a couple extra bottles so Henry can feed him too. That morning, he cleaned me out on both sides. I was also sleepy, so I decided not to pump. After changing a second diaper (within twenty minutes), I swaddled Oliver. I lay him in the crib. He was completely milk drunk, and though it felt like cheating, I tiptoed back to bed for another short sleep cycle.

The first nap of the day lasts forty minutes. I wake up to another wet diaper and a hungry baby. On average, I try to feed Oliver every two to two and a half hours, but in the mornings, he eats more frequently. So, he latches on again with his tiny plump lips and nurses for another fifteen minutes before he is awake and ready to talk to me with little coos.

I put him down again for a nap after an hour of "wake time." It's now 8:45 a.m. I whispered to Henry that Oliver was fed, changed, and going down for his second nap. Then I took a shower. I was on maternity leave but decided to get on a call with my boss two weeks before my back-to-work date to check in. I didn't want to think about work yet, but I was also eager to check in and make sure no one at the office had forgotten I exist.

After greetings, my boss and I started to talk schedule.

"I don't know if you know this, but I'll need to breastfeed or pump about every two and a half hours during the day," I said.

"I didn't know that. Wow. OK. That's pretty often."

"Yeah. It's pretty crazy. Regardless. I'll make sure my work gets done."

"I don't doubt it," he said.

"Thanks for understanding."

The phone call ended with my boss leaving the "good news" for last. My team, made up of six men and two women, decided to plan a group activity to welcome me back to work. The group activity was water rafting. The starting point of this adventure was to be about an hour and a half away from my house. While my boss shared the details of my welcoming event, I started to try to figure out how it all was going to work.

Logistically speaking, I would have to drive to the destination, pump before the three-hour excursion down river, drive back up to our cars, most likely with engorged, leaking breasts, and immediately pump when we got back to the starting point. (Assuming the recreational company taking us out on the water doesn't have a mother's room, I would most likely pump in my car before and after.)

How fun.

The activity was slated for the end of the month. I told my boss I had questions, and he let me know that Tyler from my team was planning the event. So, I was to take them up with him. Then my boss ended the call, reiterating the excitement he had for my return and the plans to celebrate it.

Afterward, it was time to feed Oliver. I told Henry about the meeting and the group activity, and he frowned.

"You should have told them you don't want to do it."

"My boss seemed really excited."

"But the activity is to welcome *you* back, right?"

"Yes."

"But it's just going to stress you out."

"Yes. I'll talk to Tyler. Maybe we can do something closer."

"They're not thinking about what that would take for you to participate."

"I didn't even know I had to feed or pump every two hours before I had a baby. They probably don't know."

"Aren't they all dads?"

"All but one."

"Tyler?"

"He has three kids."

"You should say something."

"We'll see. I have to go. I'm meeting up with Hayley now, remember? Taking Oliver."

"Good. Good. Tell her I say hi."

Reaching the top of a grassy hill after a short walk, my friend Hayley and I stopped our strollers under the shade of a large pine tree. Hayley took her daughter, Chloe, out of her bassinet on wheels. It was not long ago that I had researched every stroller on the planet, so I was well aware that Hayley's stroller was about $1,100 more expensive than my generic travel system. When I thought there could be no one paler than Hayley and her husband, their daughter had proved me wrong. Where her skin wasn't blotchy red, her skin was toothpaste white. Where it wasn't toothpaste white, it was translucent. I could have sworn I could see the fresh blood pumping through her tiny little blue veins. Lastly, Chloe was strangely broad in the strangest places, and her eyes small, along with even smaller ears. She looked at the world the way most adults look at their office space on a Monday. To be polite: she was an ugly baby.

Still, she was Hayley's third child, which meant my friend had much more experience than I had when it came to being a mother. I took Oliver out of the stroller to give him a break from the bassinet straps—and if I'm being honest, I also missed holding him in my arms. I tried to cleanse my judgmental mind as I glanced at Hayley's little goblin and reminded myself that her first daughter was now a beautiful little girl. In time, her second daughter would ripen up as well.

Hayley and I were in different lines of work, but we still had similar work things that we liked to complain about. She casually started self-expressing into a bottle, squeezing around her nipple and extracting milk. She did it with the same minimal effort and focus one might peel a banana with. She had already collected an ounce of milk before I could maneuver Oliver sideways and properly use my nipple to flirt with his lips.

"You're a natural," I said, openly staring at her chest.

"I only hand express. Feeding her directly from my boob literally hurts more than giving birth."

"I'm still getting the hang of pumping," I said. Then I accidentally sprayed my son in the eye with breast milk. The excess milk leaked from his face and my nipple onto my breast pad, bra, and tank top. "I guess I'm still getting the hang of breastfeeding too. There are no brakes on this thing."

Hayley laughed. "They have classes on birth, when a lot of it is out of your control and up to the midwives or doctors. Then you have feeding your kid, where there's a lot you can do to make things better. Labor lasts for two to forty-eight hours, and feeding your baby lasts for weeks, months, years. But feeding your kid is, like, a five-minute section in a three-day workshop."

I nodded. Oliver finally latched onto my nipple. His eyes closed while he focused on his meal. Hayley went on. "We hear about things like our water breaking and taking deep breaths . . . I don't know about you, but nobody told me about mastitis."

Four months into feeding Oliver, and I still think about that conversation with Hayley at the park. It was all true. There was so much about breastfeeding that was worth knowing. So many details that would change a mother's preparations, their day-to-day, their lives. It took an activity like water rafting from adventurous to mission impossible for a new mom. I hadn't yet pumped in my car. I'd only pumped at home. Just thinking about the logistics of the work activity again began to overwhelm me.

When I got home from my walk, Oliver went down for a short, thirty-minute nap since he slept a bit on the walk. It was 2:00 p.m. when he woke up, and Henry asked if he could feed him. We maintained about two to three bottles in the fridge at one time. Henry bottle-fed Oliver with my milk one to two times a day for a couple of reasons. First, because Henry obviously can't breastfeed, we wanted to make sure Henry experienced feeding Oliver and was able to bond with him in that way. Second, when I started work back up again in a couple of weeks, Henry would need to bottle-feed him during the busiest times of my workday, and I needed to pump that amount of milk now to make sure I would have enough in the future. If I only breastfed up to this point, it would be challenging to increase my supply suddenly when work started, so I had to trick my body into producing more to bottle up now.

What annoyed me was that even when Henry bottle-fed Oliver, I didn't get a break. I still had to pump when he fed him. Plus, it's actually more work to pump than it is to breastfeed, so it's extra time and effort to make sure Henry has the milk he needs for Oliver. Sometimes I sit on the couch next to them: me with my pump, Henry and Oliver with the bottle. On this day, I decided to go into the bedroom so that Henry and Oliver could have some alone time to bond while Oliver ate.

Before I pull the plastic to my breast, I run my hand over my chest with coconut oil. Then I start pumping, holding the flange to my areola with my left hand while I massage and express milk with my right. I only get half an ounce if I pump hands-free. I can fill a five-ounce bottle if I help massage the milk out of the ducts. The ads with a woman wearing a hands-free pump while doing the dishes or her makeup are the furthest thing from the truth. When I pump, my hands are full. There is no domesticated, wifely activity I can perform. I can't even scroll on my phone. I can't close my eyes. I focus on my breast, feeling around with the oil for any cord-like shapes that have hardened under my skin that I may need to work out.

Though my annoyance for pumping is strong, my fear of mastitis is much stronger. What is mastitis? It's inflamed breast tissue that usually involves an infection. It is a breastfeeding woman's worst nightmare. If you Google this, be warned. The image section is not for the faint of heart. (Imagine a blister the size of your breast that exists internally and externally on your chest.) It's described as terribly painful and can make one feel as if they have the flu on top of a raw, infected breast. Resolving worst-case scenarios may require surgery. After looking at breasts that are infected, I have done everything in my power to make sure my breasts avoid infection. I always search for the hard, cord-like feeling in my breasts to make sure I can massage out anything that even slightly resembles something that could lead to the terrifying infection.

By 7:00 p.m., I am feeding him for the sixth, seventh, or eighth time. This is the final feed before we put him down for the night. I always feed him in the bedroom near the crib so he can get comfortable and know it's bedtime.

Now, I know I said it was the final feed, but the real final feed is actually two or three hours later at 9:00 or 10:00 p.m. Somewhere around there. This is what we call the dream feed. I pick him up gently. He stays asleep. His eyes never open, but his mouth does. I feed him for the final time, relieving my breasts for the final time. I change his diaper again before putting him down for the night. His eyes are still closed, his hands limp.

If he doesn't drink a lot for the dream feed, I'm forced to pump. Tonight he does the job, and I get to go down for the night without having to connect a machine to my body. The more I empty out my breasts, the quicker milk fills them. It's an endless cycle, but I have to empty them out before I try to get a stretch of sleep.

To me, there are two cruel "jokes" about breastfeeding. Both of them I was unaware of before having a baby, and both realizations led to a rude awakening.

First of all, I had thought I had sleeping on my stomach to look forward to after delivering my baby. It was one of the things I was looking forward to most of all actually. I fantasized about the day I would get to return to my original sleeping habit of lying flat on my stomach on a firm mattress without a pillow in sight. Oh, how wrong I was. After giving birth, my breasts were sensitive, sore from feeding constantly and often incorrectly, and lastly, full of milk (duh). The reality is that I have about a thirty-minute window of time after Oliver or pumping completely drains me for me to lie on my stomach before my breasts start to "refill," and I have to turn onto my side. The days of stomach sleeping will have to wait until my breastfeeding days are over. Frankly, I'm not sure when that will be.

The second joke and realization was sleeping itself. Sleep deprivation was a serious issue for both me and Henry in the beginning weeks. I read seven different books on sleep training. Though most explained that sleep training doesn't work until the baby is about four to six months old, I started with Oliver when he was five weeks old. I knew if I didn't get more sleep, things could get seriously dangerous. (No parent should be allowed to even drive until their baby is eight weeks old because of this.)

The first night Oliver slept for more than two hours felt like a victory. I lay in my bed smiling. The sleep training was working. The system was working. Oliver would sleep for more than two hours eventually. He would. So would I. Or so I thought.

I remember waking up at two in the morning. Oliver was still asleep (yay!), but I wasn't. My breasts were hard, sore, throbbing, engorged, leaking. It was then that I realized that even if Oliver slept through the night, my breasts weren't getting the memo. I would still have to pump. I vaguely recall growling as I looked down at my breasts.

It was a bitter reality to swallow. One that still makes me grimace.

By the time Oliver was three months old, he was able to sleep eight to ten hours a night consistently. At four months, Oliver slept long enough to make other parents envious. But I still have to wake up to pump, and because I still have to pump, I take the night shift. This was not the plan. Henry was the night owl. I was an early riser. The morning person. Now, I roam the kitchen at two or three in the morning, fumbling for a breast flange or membrane to attach to a tube.

As I lay down Oliver after the dream feed, I bid him goodnight. I will be up in a few hours, but I won't see him until six in the morning. It is still a tender mercy, but one I still am not ready to be completely grateful for. I had thought the eight-hour stretches I once had before motherhood would return to me after our baby learned to sleep through the night. The reality was that the eight-hour stretches were still months and months away.

I hear the side-to-side rolling of my baby. I look at the clock. It's 5:55 a.m. I am tired. I sit up. Stand up. Walk over. I hover over the crib. Oliver smiles at me. He coos. He arches his back like a little kitten flirting for milk. Never has someone been so happy to see my face. I am exhausted, but I have the one thing to keep Oliver smiling. To keep him sustained. I feel joy. I take him in my arms. "Good morning," I whisper.

21

SLEEP TRAINING INSTRUCTIONS (A STEP-BY-STEP GUIDE)

1. The first step is learning about the many definitions of sleep training, including the Cry It Out method, the Ferber method, the 5 *S*'s, and more.

2. The second step includes you swearing to yourself that you will never, ever, ever let your baby cry it out. In fact, you'll say, "Over my dead body will I let my baby cry it out."

3. Over a period of weeks or months, you will find that you are, in fact, not sleeping. When you do sleep, it's hardly at all, and if you fall into the baby's trap, you might find that the baby is actually eating more often in the night than in the day. Then you might notice that they've become very attached. So attached to you that they can sense when you're about to let go of them. They start to cry just from you thinking about the idea of setting them down in their crib.

4. This is when your partner, the one who is not breastfeeding, will either tell you to "feed them already" so you both can get another hour or two of sleep before your baby wakes up again, demanding another comfort

feed, *or* they will raise an eyebrow at you and in an accusatory tone ask, "Well, I wonder why they're just *so* attached to you all of the time?" Or maybe, in a more playful tone (which still maintains the accusation), they'll say, "They have you wrapped around their finger, you know that?"

5. Step five is simple and will come naturally (mainly from the sleep deprivation). You will break. And you will ask your pediatrician about sleep training, and they will smile and say, "The first three days are hard, and then it is wonderful." Sleep training will mean two things: it will be the Cry It Out method, and it will lead to more sleep for you, your partner, and your baby.

6. The first night will consist of preparations. Anxiously you'll arrange the crib so that it's as comfortable for baby as possible. This will consist of really rearranging nothing because there's nothing but a fitted crib sheet that can be put in the crib for safe sleep. That's when you realize there is no comfort that you can offer your baby while you're away.

7. After the last feed and burp, you lay your baby down. They will be upset, and their cry will sound like, "What are you doing, Mama? Why are you betraying me so?"

8. In another room, you hold the baby monitor tightly in your fingers. You can hear your baby. You can see your baby. You blink. Your partner asks, "Do you want to sleep downstairs, and I'll take the monitor?" You say no. Because if your baby must suffer, you must suffer.

9. When you first hear your baby, you will regret your decision. You will renounce the need for sleep and stand up and rush the door. Your partner will stop you, and you will hate them for it. They will hate you for hating them

for it, and the amount of hatred felt will depend solely on the intensity of the cries coming through the door.

10. You guess it might have been two hours of crying as you sit there listening to your child. You look at the stopwatch that you started since the cries began. It has not been two hours. It has been six and a half minutes, and you know you cannot do it.

11. *PleaseDearGod. PleaseDearGod. Go to sleep. Stop crying. I cannot help you. Go to sleep. Go to sleep. Dear god.* You chant in your head to try and drown out the wailing.

12. Your partner is quiet, not calm. Stressed, not relaxed, Strong, not weak. You are weak. You are crying, and now you have doomed your child, for how can you ask them to stop crying if you can't?

13. After thirty-five minutes, your baby's volumes are exhausted, and your baby falls asleep. You are bothered by the fact that their sheet may be wet from the tears, that their nose is plastered with wet mucousy, abandoned boogers. But you are comforted by the fact that they are asleep and no longer weeping. It is a compromise.

14. You wake up. You're startled. Your baby is stirring. What time is it? Your baby is not crying but awake. They have been asleep for ten and a half hours straight.

15. You realize all at once that the Cry It Out method works and that you're fucked because you have two more nights of this, if not more, before the training really sets in.

22

LESS KOREAN

As you know, when I became pregnant for the second time, it was shortly after we had experienced our first miscarriage. After checking for the 109th time that I was, indeed, pregnant again, Henry and I decided we wanted to wait until the baby came to find out the gender (as you also know). There were a few reasons we did this.

First, when I was pregnant the first time, we were both so sure it was a girl—our little Ava. We started talking to *her* and planning for *her,* and when we lost *her* . . . Well, there are no words. We simply lost *her*. Thinking back, not knowing a gender for the second pregnancy wouldn't have made the loss any less tough. But we were pulling out all the stops to fight off heartbreak should we lose another baby.

Second, we were so beyond happy when we found out we were pregnant again that we didn't care to know. We only cared that we had a healthy baby on the way.

Third, we didn't want pink everything or blue everything. We wanted the world to be flexible and full of options for our baby, and not knowing the gender naturally helped with that. We got a lot of, "But how will we know what to buy for your baby?" questions, and somehow, they all figured it out in the end without knowing the gender.

Fourth, we decided that we wanted a surprise. It's not often you get a surprise like this as an adult. So, we would give this surprise to ourselves, from ourselves.

Now, the further we got into our pregnancy, the desire to know the gender grew. At one point it was nearly unbearable! I wanted to know so desperately and almost gave in several times. But even more than the gender, I just wanted to know what my baby looked like. Henry's family is made up of mostly blue-eyed, fair-skinned folks. Would my baby have blue eyes? Would their skin be pale? Would their hair be light? And then the deep, burning questions from my core: Would my baby look Asian? With only a quarter Korean blood in them, would they look at all Korean? Would my baby look . . . like me?

Late in my second and third trimester with Oliver, I had several dreams in which I saw my baby. It was a girl with blue eyes and dark hair. Other than the blue eyes, she actually looked nearly identical to Oliver. (It's only now, writing this, that I wonder if that was the baby we lost. If that was Ava.) I wondered about that baby in my dreams. Was she who we would meet? Was that what our baby would look like?

I worried that our baby wouldn't look Asian for two reasons mainly.

The first reason was simply the fear of losing my already distant and fading heritage. I had grown up half-Korean, and in Utah no less, and that led to experiences that left me confused—albeit proud—and frustrated.

The confusion stemmed more from the unknown of

my mother's culture. She had experienced some terrible violence that she left in South Korea, and she didn't talk much about her childhood or upbringing. I only had bits to piece together from when she opened up on the rare occasion. My mother's country, always present in her round eyes, thick, dark hair, and kimchi breath, always felt out of reach. To add to that feeling, both of my parents spoke Korean. My American father had lived in Seoul for seven years. But when my mother flew to Utah with my dad to take care of my paternal grandpa who had grown ill, my dad forced her to speak English.

"No more Korean. You're in America now."

Once my mother was speaking English fluently, my parents spoke Korean when they didn't want us to understand what they were saying. Yet, we were able to pick up on things. My sisters would protest that they actually hadn't gained weight when my dad mumbled something to my mom in the kitchen. You don't need to know a language to know when you're being judged. Still to this day, when I hear the language, my first instinct is to check myself and wonder what is "wrong" about me. Have I gained weight? Did I get too much sun? Did I sleep in and waste the day? What is being said critically about me?

Still, everything that was connected to my mother's side drew me in. As a child, there was nothing more alluring than where she came from.

I loved my mother's cooking growing up. I still remember the meals I had when I was so small my mother had to spoon feed me: rice and seaweed soup, kimbap, turnip, butter rice and water kimchi, cucumber kimchi, fried fish, brown potatoes, black beans, bean sprouts. Mmm, all of it.

Growing up in southern Utah, we'd make trips to Las

Vegas every one or two months so my mother could bulk shop at the Asian supermarket and cook her traditional Korean dishes for us all to enjoy in one of the whitest states in the country. I distinctly remember the ads I would see hanging up in those stores. Looking at the faces in the skincare section was like looking at glowing princesses. I'd never seen such beautiful humans before. I would stare in awe as my mom put a small pack of Pocky sticks in my hand to snack on for the drive home. Before we would leave, I'd also try to stop in the kitchenware section. I loved looking at the vibrant-patterned bowls, the intricate designs of the chopsticks, all of the colors that shone under the fluorescent light, revealing dragons or leaves intertwined with flowers. It was a magical place where all of these lucky people got to shop for their everyday essentials regularly. I envied all of them.

Before crossing the state border and heading home, we always made a second stop to eat KBBQ (Korean BBQ). It was the one time every month or two that my mother didn't have to cook Korean food for herself to eat it. She always ordered the best dishes, and I loved trying the new things she didn't make herself. To this day, I still have never seen any man or woman of any size eat more than my 106-pound mother at a KBBQ restaurant.

I also always looked forward to the reactions of the servers when they heard my father speak Korean. He absolutely lived for looking at the menu and pretending to seem confused, just waiting for them to mutter something of impatience under their breath. Then he'd come in swinging with a joke in their language, and the server's face would melt into a dazed shock. My father loved it, and I thought it was the most hilarious thing to watch as a child. I'd always giggle when they made their faces of surprise.

I loved the Korean music videos that would play on the TVs while we ate. They were always soft, tragic love stories told in slow motion. I would be eating bulgogi thinking, "If only he knew she was still alive!" or, "If only she wasn't blind and could see it was him all along!" It was Romeo and Juliet told through characters in a language I couldn't understand, over and over again. Perhaps that's why I'm so dramatic and tragic sometimes about my own life.

As enchanted as I was by the music videos, skincare posters, and side dishes, this culture—my culture—often felt quite irrelevant. Growing up in a small town, I often forgot I was different at all. I felt as white as Britney, Brittany, and Britneigh.

Growing up—and still today—there are moments of ignorance. (I find in Utah, especially, it's often ignorance more than it is maliciousness.) I've seen people press their fingers to the corners of their eyes and pull them wide to make their eyes smaller—and honestly really don't feel anything when they do. I still often hear the term "oriental" to describe others. It wasn't until I actually went to college when I learned that oriental was supposed to be used to describe objects and not people. I often read in novels that an Asian character's eyes are almond-shaped and that someone that might look like me has skin the color of brown sugar. I'm rather indifferent to all of those descriptions and gestures. In fact, I'm quite unbothered.

However, I loved (and still love) being different. I loved my name and the presence and connection it had to Asian cultures. I loved turning brown instead of pink under the sun. I loved standing out in a place like Utah while being able to blend into countries in multiple continents.

When people ask me where I'm from, one of those ignorant but not quite malicious questions, I'm proud to tell them my mother is from Seoul. I like that they know there's something about me that begged that question. Still to this day, similar to the term "oriental," I don't mind when someone asks what my ethnicity is or where I'm from. I'm happy to let them know I was born in Utah of all places but that my mom's side is South Korean. It truly doesn't bother me—though I understand why it would seem rather otherish and exhaustive to others.

While "almond-shaped eyes" might be a rather overused description from a writing perspective, I'd say it is often accurate. And being described to have skin the color of brown sugar actually sounds like flattery to me. Oftentimes, when people who look like me are outraged, I don't feel the same. I feel quite ... fine. I once had a friend who was livid that a Korean dish had been turned into a burrito on YouTube. She took to social media, pointing fingers at a chef who had dared blend bibimbap with a tortilla. I simply wanted to try the burrito. Sometimes I wonder if I don't feel this outrage because I'm only half. Because I'm not whole. Maybe I don't know any better. Maybe I'm my own kind of ignorant. I'm not sure. But I don't think how I feel is wrong. It's just different.

Today, when I walk into a new place—a coffee shop, a yoga class, a boutique—I immediately note if there are other people of color in the room. I didn't realize I did this until a few years ago. I had been doing it ever since I moved to Salt Lake City. At any point in time, I would tell my husband, "Look. There are three other Asian women in here," or something of the like, until he pointed it out.

"You always know how many non-white people are wherever we are," he observed.

He was right. At any given time, I just knew. I don't know if this is one-sided on my end, but I immediately feel a connection with others who look like me. I immediately feel an energy. I feel . . . an understanding. Maybe even a power, and I feel proud. Though the big cities I have lived in aren't for me, I miss not having to involuntarily count the others in the room. And whenever I visit a big city, that's one of the first things that brings a smile to my face. Nothing about me stands out when everything and everyone is so loud, so colorful, so vibrant. Sometimes blending in by being a part of the rainbow is the best feeling.

Will my child know this feeling?

But also, when I encounter other Koreans and that connection is made, what comes next always makes me want to apologize. If our encounter goes beyond a smile and nod, it means they're approaching and greeting me in Korean. All I can offer is the shortest form of "hello" in Korean as a response, and then my knowledge of the language ends (unless they're interested in hearing me list off the most popular menu items that are typically found on a KBBQ menu). Our connection is frozen. I can't receive their words, and I immediately see their faces change. I feel them withdraw.

Will they withdraw from my child too?

This happens often in other languages too. Strangers approach and greet me in Spanish, along with a range of Asian languages like Mandarin, Japanese, Filipino, Thai, and the list goes on. I always have to raise my hand in surrender and explain to them that I don't speak their language. But when it's Korean, I have to apologize for the fact that I don't speak *my* language. Most often after those encounters, I vow to learn the language and speak fluently. I've gone so far as to teach myself the alphabet, and I'm able to sound out words on my own. However, that's as far as I've gotten, and I'm forgetting quickly.

I usually talk myself out of it. *How often will I actually use the language? Shouldn't I put time into learning how to draw, or play an instrument, or learn Spanish? Technology will be so advanced that by the time I actually learn to speak Korean, we'll have instant, in-person translation thanks to creepy and yet undeniable AI.*

I think about what languages I could help my future child learn. Should I finally commit to learning Korean and learn with them? They will be a quarter Korean, perhaps they'll be even more motivated to make their connection to their Korean heritage stronger. *Or I could teach them a language they'll use more often...*

If you recall from many, many words ago, there was a second reason I was worried that my child wouldn't look Korean. This reason is very selfish, but I worried that if I birthed a blonde-haired, or even sandy-haired, boy or girl with blue eyes, would I feel a connection to them? I had heard about mothers who had babies that *did* look like them and still did not feel any connection or attachment to their babies from the beginning, and I was slightly worried about that just in general.

But if my child didn't look like me, but looked like another Britney, would I feel that motherly love that I hoped to God would kick in when I was running on two hours of sleep in the first seventy-two hours of their lives? When my breasts were so swollen and full of milk that I could easily mistake them for giant blistering boils on my chest? What about then? What if I didn't feel love for my child because they looked ... not like me?

A few notes around this concern now that Oliver has arrived:

First, my child looks exactly as I would have imagined. I immediately recognized myself in him. He has dark, dark brown hair and nearly black eyes. Even in the first few days of life, I could tell his skin wasn't fair or porcelain. It could be described in that jaded, or maybe offensive, way as cinnamon. In those first days, I didn't actually really see Henry in him at all. (Though, every day that passes, he takes on more Henry, and nowadays, all I see is Henry and Henry Jr.) So, the worry was all for nothing.

Second, even though Oliver looked like me and his Asianness was strongly present, he still looked more like a naked mole rat and behaved more like a potato. To say that I felt connected to him right away—though I didn't feel *not* connected to him—feels like a stretch.

Did I love him? I didn't know him. I would have died for him—for I understood that he was my son. But the love I feel for him now—that feeling of tension, and release, and dread, and ecstasy when I see him lose his balance from giggling while sitting? That wasn't there before. Or perhaps it was there, but like a seed. Small and delicate, with the potential to grow into a one-hundred-year-old oak or shrivel up into a terminal and raisin-like crumb. It grew into this beautiful love plant after each day we spent together, and it still grows on the sad days and the hard days, just like it does the happy days and the good days. (Spoiler: there are no easy days.)

Third, to conclude, my child looks like me. And I'm glad he does. However, if he didn't, I think the seed I worried about would grow all the same: day by day.

So, all this rambling, and yet I still wonder as I look at this little, quarter-Korean baby boy of mine:

Will knowing BTS and KBBQ be enough?

When you're older, will ignorant but fascinated people ask you where you're from?

If you don't tolerate spicy food, will Harmony (할머니) make fun of you too?

Should we learn Korean together?

Would you prefer a more practical language?

But as I reflect on my relationship with my parents, and my father specifically—a man who I've spoken fewer than ten words to in the last few years—I tell my son as he stacks blocks in our upstairs attic:

Whatever language you speak, I will be here, and I will listen.

23

I HAVE WRITTEN NOTHING

I sit in the kitchen listening to your cries. They come deep from your chest and through your lungs, but they are not loud because you are wearing yourself out from the two hours that have passed. Are you teething? Is there gas and pressure in your stomach? Is the diaper too tight? Is this the five-month regression? Are you not full from the first two feedings (but you ate so well!)?

Henry holds you. Rocks you. I want to come to you, but Henry doesn't want me to.

"I don't need help," he says.

But I'm not coming to help *him*. I'm coming to help *you*. Your cries pull at me. Each cry, each sob, each wail, pulls a layer from my core, and those layers do not come easy. They are torn away, painfully like fresh skin raw. My breasts throb. My throat swells. My eyes pulse. I will split in half if you continue. Henry cannot know this pain. Only I know this pain. I want my baby. I want to soothe you. I know I can calm you.

But Henry holds you. He rocks you. He doesn't need my help, and he is your father.

So, I sit here in front of my laptop in the kitchen. I try to do something. Anything. I try to write. But I have written nothing. Nothing. Nothing. And I am tearing into pieces, away.

24

MILKY DREAMS

There were two outings—despite breastfeeding—that I went on in the first six months of Oliver's life that are worth noting.

The Work Trip

I found out about the work trip in a team meeting.

"You're all going to love it. Three days in San Francisco. We'll fly everyone in and out and get a hotel, so we're all staying in the same place. Now, we'll be discussing big projects for the new year, but we'll also be extremely focused on team bonding. (Get ready for karaoke!)"

Did I think about staying and missing the three-day work trip? Of course I did. That was my first thought. But if I stayed, I wouldn't be a part of the conversations around the projects for the new year. I'd get the chopped liver of projects that no one wanted. When it came to team bonding, I would be one large face on a large screen calling in remotely, and the big projects, promotions, and other opportunities would go to my colleagues: Sam,

Chris, and Mark. I would be—albeit unintentionally—forgotten. No. I couldn't let that happen. I would do it. I would go.

And go I did.

I flew in on Tuesday night. It was the first bedtime of Oliver's I had missed since he was born. Henry would be trying to put him to sleep with a bottle I had pumped a few weeks earlier. I hadn't been producing more milk than I needed to, so as soon as I found out about the work trip, I had to double the time I spent pumping in order to increase my milk supply and barely scrape by with enough milk to freeze for the three-day trip. Did you know a six-month-old drinks about thirty-two ounces of milk a day?

When I sat in the hotel that night at 7:30 p.m., I regretted not having Henry do a few of the bedtime routines without me completely while I was at home. Just Henry, Oliver, the bottle, and our bedtime story. Then I wouldn't have to sit on the bed in the dark, wondering if Oliver was settling. Wondering if Henry felt overwhelmed or totally cool. There was no way to know, and what was the point? What could I do here in my hotel room in San Francisco?

I got invited to a dinner with Sam, Chris, and Mark. But my boss and the others hadn't arrived, so I decided to pass on the bonding with the colleagues I saw every day and instead take advantage of alone time. Let me tell you, it wasn't like riding a bike.

First, I unpacked. I owned a small carry-on that I used to take for weekend trips and short business trips like this, but I had to buy a brand-new suitcase for this trip. My older suitcase couldn't fit what I needed with all of my pumping supplies, and I wasn't even worried about storage. I could have arranged to freeze my milk at the hotel or ship it to Henry, but I couldn't wrap my mind around it. So, all of the glorious, pumped milk from the next three days would be dumped out for the sole reason of keeping up my milk supply for Oliver when I got home.

I took a hot shower and then said fuck it and took a bath. I then proceeded to order room service—something I had never done—and watched *Friends* reruns while dipping a fry multiple times into a small bowl of ketchup.

Henry called me at 10:00 p.m. and confirmed that Oliver was well aware that Mama was nowhere to be found, but two and a half hours later, he had gone down. We chatted. Henry was exhausted. I felt guilty I wasn't there to help. We both knew the night wasn't going to get better, and our one consolation was the alone time we were keeping each other from. So, we said our goodnights and "I love yous," and then I cried myself to sleep.

I was proud to show my face in California. To show everyone that I could do work trips too. I wore a light blazer over a company shirt and jeans. I also wanted to show that I could wear jeans. Everyone asked about my baby, and I smiled and told them Oliver was great. Inside, I wanted to say I also wondered about my baby. That I wondered what he was doing right now. I wondered if he was hungry. I wondered if his father needed help. I wondered why I was on this stupid trip.

I never wondered about all of those things more than every two hours when I had to awkwardly break away from the chain of presentations that had allowed for five-to-ten-minute breaks every two to three hours to pump. I sat in a plain room in a chair, pumping to dump. Looking at photos of Oliver and wondering and wondering and wondering. I did not pump very much, and I wondered if it was because of a matter-of-fact reason, like Oliver at six months old was much better and more efficient at emptying me out than a lifeless machine was, or if it was something more visceral, like my heart wasn't in it, so the milk didn't come.

All in all, I missed about two hours of huddles, workshops, and presentations, and only to dump the milk too. After work, everyone headed to a bar and restaurant that had been rented out for the gathering. I gave myself one last pumping session, and then I attended because, one, I was hungry, and two, I wanted to get as much face time with the people responsible for promoting me in the coming months, and maybe even years, as possible. I was rusty, but it felt good to get out. A lot of the people out that night were parents. They all seemed so much more relaxed than I did. Was it just me turning into a tight ball of anxiety the longer I was away? What was wrong with me?

I listened to my boss and my boss's boss talk about the next marathon they were going to run together. I still couldn't even use our stationary bike because my hemorrhoids were so terrible, and the thought of running or even taking the stairs up too fast made my breasts scream. I listened to their ambitions in awe.

That night—night two away from my family—Henry called about the same time. Oliver didn't take as long to go down but was definitely missing Mama—his words, not mine. We said goodnight and I love you. That night I did not cry, and I slept through the night for the first time in at least a year.

I woke up feeling refreshed. But what did feeling refreshed really matter when the breast parts—excuse me—best parts of you are missing?

It's one of those things that's hard to explain to someone who doesn't have kids.

I'm so tired, I haven't slept through a night in a year.
 Then get a hotel away from the baby and get a good night's sleep.
 But then I'm away from the baby.
 So . . . what's the problem?

Yeah. I know. It doesn't make sense. But that's just how it is. You'll never be rested and have a full heart, and you'll never have a full heart and feel rested. Something like that. I was too irritated to think about if that was actually right.

When I woke up the next morning, it was just a travel day. Like the last morning that I was away from my family, my sunrise started with hooking up to my pumping machine and listening to the rhythmic suction that caused my nipples to stretch and feel raw for the next couple of hours—a feeling which would wear off just before it was time to pump again. We all ate breakfast at the hotel and headed out. I pumped once more in the airport restrooms, dumped again, and was off.

When we landed, I should have pumped, but I was too tired from the trip and too excited to see my family. I took an Uber straight to my house.

When I got home, I felt so much relief. One, because I was so happy to see my family, and two, because Oliver literally relieved me by latching on immediately and emptying me out the way a machine could never do. Henry lay next to me on the bed as I fed our son. He held my hand with his left hand and covered his eyes with his right hand, giving into sleep.

The Spa Day

I had been craving a full spa day for a long time but was too anxious to leave Oliver. I finally decided it was time, but logistically, with breastfeeding, it was challenging. I stubbornly wanted to do more than just a massage. I wanted to do an Ofuro bath before a massage and then a facial after. I wanted a long, pampering break, which meant about four and a half hours away from the house and baby, including the drive.

Nearly five hours straight without feeding Oliver meant pumping, so I packed my bag accordingly. Pumping Machine. Pumping Tube. Plumbing bottles and their attachments. Small cooler with ice packs. Storage bottles. Towels. The works.

On the day of luxury, I fed Oliver right before I stepped out the door with my duffel bag of equipment. I checked into the spa and settled into a nice, long forty-five-minute bath. An hour later, I found myself lying face down on a massage table. I realized suddenly that my breasts had been fuller than expected from the warm bath and that lying on my stomach was actually quite painful even though it had only been an hour and fifteen minutes since I fed my son. I awkwardly had to explain to my massage therapist that I needed to lie on my side. We used a few pillows. The massage was OK, but not what it used to be.

After the massage, I had allowed time to officially pump before my facial. It was awkward to decide where to pump. Did I do it literally in a stall over a toilet, or should

I settle in the locker room and be drained while middle-aged women undressed in front of me? Distance from the toilet won out, and I ended up worrying about having to deal with women walking in on my pumping, when only one older woman walked in and was luckily stationed across the way from me. I didn't even have to face her while pumping.

I went into my facial emptied out as much as possible. Still not as empty as I would be if Oliver were there. As I lay down while the technician smothered what seemed to be banana pudding over my face, I began to strategize ways that I could get Henry and Oliver to make a trip out there next time so that I could feed him directly without having to pump. I could space out the services an hour in between so I could leave the facility, feed Oliver in the car, and then go back in for the next service. But would Henry just wait outside the whole time? Would they drive back and forth each hour? Could he bring Oliver in, or were babies frowned upon in fancy spas? It wouldn't work. What could I do?

Then my facial was over, and I was left without a solution for the future. When I got home, I found the classic facial I had always gotten had irritated my skin. My sensitivities to things on my face had been heightened since pregnancy, and this was no different. I did not come home glowing. I came home with a redness at the scalp that Henry avoided commenting on. He only kissed me to welcome me home before handing Oliver off so he could have his five-hour video game splurge.

Day of luxury indeed.

Now, I have to confess. At the beginning of this chapter, I said the following:

There were two outings—despite breastfeeding—that I went on in the first six months of Oliver's life that are worth noting.

Well, I lied. I had these two opportunities to go out: a work trip in San Francisco and a spa day for myself. But I thought about how it would go, detailing it out moment by moment as you read above. And it was too much. I couldn't do it while breastfeeding. It was too overwhelming to think about, let alone do.

I didn't go to San Francisco. I did not go to the spa. I stayed home. I fed Oliver. I did not leave the ship at the port but rather stayed on the boat, anchored by the weight of what three days or even five hours away from my little one would entail. And did I feel relieved to have stayed? Yes. Happy even? Yes. Did I feel sad to have stayed? Well, also yes.

25

THE WHY

When I first met Henry, I was working multiple odd jobs: a barista in the morning, a waitress at lunch and dinner, and the library on the weekends. He held one steady job that started at nine and ended at five. When I started my first nine-to-five job, it felt like I was giving up on my freedom. Maybe even my childhood. I had always wanted to be a writer, and committing so many hours a day to not being a writer felt like I had turned my back on my dreams.

I was twenty-four when I started my first job as a technical writer for a manufacturing company. After a year, I had moved into marketing in another industry, which was more my speed. By the time Henry and I got married, I was in a manager position and encouraged Henry to take a break from work and go back to school to get his bachelor's degree. He had had a rough go as an eighteen-year-old freshman, and he had been pining over a degree ever since dropping out. After a year of deliberation, he finally quit his job—just shy of a decade of manual labor at the same company. He started going to school full-time in the midst of the pandemic and continued his education when it was moved exclusively online.

Ever since I started my first office job, I've told my husband, "Don't hold your breath. I'm sure I'll be fired tomorrow . . ." Yet, I have only continued to be promoted and recognized in my career. By the time I was pregnant, I was a director, and Henry was only twenty credits away from graduating with his own degree in English. Despite my constant desire to be a stay-at-home mom, and Henry's desire to have an office to commute to each morning, logistically, it simply made more sense for me to continue to work and for Henry to continue with school and become the primary caretaker.

It has taken a while to get to this place in my life where I have accepted that the majority of the hours in my day are spent working in a job I am not passionate about. That most words that I write don't give me pleasure and are not for me or for a special reader looking for an escape but rather for a business where my main goal is to sell more things. (Perhaps that's why I write so well when it comes to work. I find it easier to write when I'm detached from the topic.) Even before we started our little family, I had slowly accepted that after 5:00 p.m. on weekdays and Saturdays and Sundays are for me and what I actually care about.

It just so happens that what I actually care about is no longer what it used to be. It's suddenly much . . . more. On LinkedIn, the social media platform for "professionals," a lot of the people simply call this "the Why." Let me explain.

Every now and then I see a man share a photo on LinkedIn of his family (without fail, it is always a family photo) and a statement on how the image is "the Why" behind why he shows up to work each day. These photos —all different families but the same photo, really— consist of the man himself, his wife, and then his children. The long curls of the wife glistening in the sun, usually holding a young infant or toddler in the warmth of her arms. Because it's Utah, there are usually three or four more children surrounding the man and his wife, all with identical hair color. It becomes a wholesome collage of spiked hair, a missing tooth, pigtails or braids ...

I always look at these photos and find it ironic that "the Why" is so, *so* important, and yet we spend the majority of our lives away from it. Away from them. It is generally acceptable that we interact with "the Why" in the evenings and on weekends. Thanks to the strange platform LinkedIn has become, it is even encouraged that we share an image of "the Why" with our colleagues to show that there is, in fact, a reason we spend most of our time sitting bent over a desk and screen all day. Perhaps the working community feels the need to post "the Why" to get the comments that justify this painful but generally accepted way of life.

Before having Oliver, if I were to post a photo of "the Why" on LinkedIn, it might look like a spontaneous shopping spree for candles at Anthropologie; a meal that charges a steep fee for its ambiance rather than the food itself; or hell, maybe even a hazy photo of a villa in the South of France that I'm vacationing in for the month of July.

Now that I have a baby, my photo would also be of the family I hope to provide for. This includes providing the necessities of life, like food, water, and shelter, but I'd also like to spoil them excessively. Outrageously. Uncontrollably.

So, what am I writing about now? What's the problem? Where's the conflict? What is this part of the book about?

Well, as I sit here, breastfeeding my little boy every two hours for about twenty minutes at a time, I think about the inevitable. Returning to work. All of the sort of big questions I've asked myself before—they have more weight to them. Questions like: Am I doing something that makes me happy? Am I creating something that I'm proud of? Am I a part of something that truly matters?

I have always asked these questions, and I've answered them in ways that aren't ideal but also are very practical. But now these questions have more weight to them because they're all tied to this new little child of mine that begs the big question: Am I setting a good example of living a fulfilling life for my son, or am I showing him through my choices that money is more important than doing something I care about?

I care about my son more than anything. I care about raising him with love more than anything, and that's why I couldn't work fifty hours a week to pay someone else to do what I care most about. That's why Henry is the primary caretaker and watching over our son. Somehow, even that situation mocks me because Henry wants to work. I want to be with our son full-time. (Or does he only say he wishes he was back in the workforce because society has us so fucked backward that he wants what he's expected to want?)

While all of these questions float in my mind, I have pushed myself harder to not bail on work the first second I get: Don't I want to show my son that women can be the "breadwinner"? (I hate that term—"winner" implies that there are also losers.) Don't I want to show my son that I'm a strong, independent woman? Don't I want to sit back and laugh while I casually drop that I put his father through school as the sole provider for our family while simultaneously giving birth to a human being?

Fine. I can still work. But can I face myself and the fact that I sacrificed time with my son—arguably the most precious and valued time of my life—to spend hours doing something I could care less about? If I'm going to continue working, continue spending time away from the Why for the Why, I'm convinced then that I need the work to matter. To mean something to me. To honor the sacrifice of not being there full-time for my son. And that is no small sacrifice.

Yes. It's decided then. I'll either stay at home and be the loving, nurturing, adventurous mother I have always dreamed of being with my son, *or* I'll quit my job and dedicate my sacrificial hours away from my son to a career writing about the shit I want to write. That's what I must do. Yes!

It's decided.

. . . But then there are things that are undone—not decided: Who will pay the mortgage? Who will pay for Henry's tuition? Who will pay for groceries? Who will spoil the family with excessive, unnecessary gifts "just because"?

My return-to-work date is August 29. I have eight more uninterrupted weeks left with the Why.

Nothing is decided.

26

BAY STEPS

Day 1 (Postpartum)

👎 I could not walk and had to be pushed in a wheelchair while I held Oliver in my arms.

👍 Oliver was born, and after waiting ten months, we learned the gender of the baby.

Day 3

👎 The doctor squeezed Oliver's heel to collect enough drops of blood to fill a small vial. Oliver cried. I cried harder.

👍 We got the last available blue-light therapy machine delivered to our house to beam away our baby's jaundice.

Day 9

👎 I bled through five heavy pads.

👍 I am only seven pounds over my pre-pregnancy weight.

. . .

Day 11

👎 Henry accidentally ripped off what was left of Oliver's umbilical cord at 11 p.m. I have never seen my husband look sorrier.

👍 A quick Google search showed he's not the only parent to accidentally yank off what was left of the mother, albeit dry and shriveled.

Week 2

👎 Oliver farted, and it scared him into a furious cry.

👍 I realized that if I didn't know what a fart was, it would terrify me too. I've never been so torn between boisterous laughter and soothing tones. So, I offered both to him.

Week 8

👎 Oliver took two hours to calm down and fall asleep, starting exactly at 6 p.m., and I came back to a cold dinner.

👍 Oliver smiled when he saw my face after he woke up for a diaper change.

Week 10

👎 Oliver had a blowout on the custom-made onesie I ordered that says "Grandma" on it.

👍 Dad's diaper songs are working, and getting his diaper changed seems to be a favorite pastime of Oliver's now. (Oh, and it looks like I'm starting to call Henry "Dad" now.)

Week 16
🌱 Oliver started screeching. Which was cute at first. Not so much the fifty-sixth time at four in the morning.

🌿 Oliver discovered his toes, and it's the most adorable show in all of the land.

Week 18
🌱 Why isn't Oliver sleeping? Did he forget all of our training? Oh, God. Is this the four-to-five-month sleep regression?

🌿 Oliver started to say the "Ma" sound. And when he repeats it over and over again like he does, he's saying, "MaMaMaMaMa," which is obviously "Mama," and now he has total power over me.

Week 20
🌱 Oliver is very good at grabbing things and putting them in his mouth—and now Mom and Dad have to hide all of the things he could choke on.

🌿 Oliver will start eating solid foods soon, and I'm really enjoying research on nutritional solid foods for babies. What will his first food be?

Week 24
🌱 I only have a few months left to breastfeed Oliver.

🌿 I only have a few months left to breastfeed Oliver.

27

GUEST CONTRIBUTOR

Having my two children was the hardest thing I have ever done. It nearly destroyed my marriage, myself, my life. All of the photos of my babies when they're six months or younger are locked away. Whenever I see an image of them that young, I only think of how miserable I was. I love them to death. Ha. Ha. But if I see a photo of them in diapers, I'll burn it.

28

MUST GET BETTER

Oliver was a week shy of eight months when he first got sick.

I would say that we were rather timid when it came to outings. We had taken him to some busy places with lots of people, like the natural history museum, the botanical gardens, and the aquarium, and we had him meet family and friends but asked everyone to wash their hands and not to kiss the baby—though the latter was a tough rule for grandparents to remember.

It started with a very small cough that lasted only a couple minutes in the morning. That cough went on for three weeks, like a flame before it grew to a fire. We did "Christmas" with Henry's family a week before the actual holiday, with plans to head to my mother's afterwards. Christmas with Henry's family was everything an old family holiday should be. There were multiple proteins—elk shot from an actual hunt, roast beef, and honeyed ham. Canned corn. Canned beans. Canned cranberries. And of course, a salad that was actually a dessert made of Jello and Cool Whip but somehow still called a salad.

There was a craft for an activity after dinner and a small gift exchange with extra presents for Oliver and his cousins.

Oliver took that holiday cheer—and a dormant cold that would flare up three days later—with us to my mother's house.

When Oliver first showed he had an actual cold, I came to the cruel realization of how little I knew of what to do in such a situation. Yes, I had read sleeping books. Yes, I had watched videos on how he should consume solid food and how to perform CPR afterward. I had taken the prenatal classes with Henry where we learned prenatal care, where we—in short—learned how not to kill our baby, but that was really as far as the class had gone.

What to do now that our sweet baby was sick? I knew very little. In fact, I knew only four things before going into the mess.

1. It was always terrible, and the younger they were, the more miserable.

2. Steam showers helped a cough.

3. Keeping baby hydrated was key.

4. Fever or trouble breathing meant it was time to go to the hospital.

In these essays, I can never say, "There will come a time where you will be watching the collarbone and chest of your baby and need to be able to tell the difference between a congested-but-okay breathing pattern and a pattern that is not OK." I can't say that because I am not experienced enough to tell you what will happen to you if and when you have a child.

But there came a time for us. Henry and I held our little boy in our arms. We weren't monitoring our child; we were examining our child as if we had never seen a baby before. Did he feel hot? Did he have a fever? Was his color all right? Why were his cheeks so red? Was he breathing OK? Was he just congested? How congested is too congested? The cough sounded bad. What if he had pneumonia, or COVID, or RSV, and we were just sitting there ... looking at him?

Then the vomiting started. The first time was probably the most vomit I had ever seen. The coughing fits spurred the vomiting, and my baby went from crying to coughing to vomiting to smiling. Those smiles. They were the only somewhat reassuring thing about the matter. Was he trying to tell us that he was OK despite it all, or was he a baby and too ignorant to know that smiles don't usually follow throwing up?

Then the coughing and vomiting became fits, and the fits caused our little boy to seize up. Finally, Henry took the keys from the table and told me to grab my coat. It was time to go to urgent care. I threw on my coat and packed the diaper bag with random items that seemed right: diapers, swaddle blankets, a children's book, a Binky, and a burp blanket. My mother said we were too paranoid as we headed out her front door. The stress was like a thick fog around us the entire way to the hospital; the entire time we filled out the questionnaire the receptionist gave us; and the entire time we sat in the clinical room with a large patient chair for children and two chairs for adults.

The first thing the doctor did was check his lungs.

"That's good," he said. "No pneumonia or RSV. Lungs sound good."

The second thing he checked was Oliver's ears.

"Not so good. He has an infection. In each ear."

"Is that what's causing the breathing issues?" Henry asked.

"No, but it's certainly not helping."

We walked out of the center with Oliver's first prescription. Sudafed and amoxicillin. We stopped at two pharmacies with the doctor's note, and both were out. From a friend's suggestion, we looked for baby Tylenol as well, but there wasn't any. There was a shortage in our state. By the time we had driven to a third pharmacy, it was closed. Every pharmacy in the small town my mother lived in was closed. It was only 8:00 p.m. I'm sure Henry was thinking what I was thinking: how there were plenty of pharmacies open where we lived. In a bigger city. With more resources. Neither of us said it though.

In the morning, Mia kindly offered to go find Oliver's medication while we kept Oliver upright and near the humidifier we had purchased the night before. She came back with both medications. The cough syrup was clear in a red bottle, and the amoxicillin for Oliver's ear infection was in a cylindrical bottle with a thick, white liquid that resembled the kind of glue children use in preschool. She also gave us a wide dropper to insert into Oliver's mouth to distribute the medicine.

Oliver did not like the dropper being poked into his little mouth. He did not like the medicine. I can't be sure if it was the taste he didn't like, or the cold he didn't like, or the way we had to hold his head still and keep his arms down he didn't like, or the way it made him cough that he didn't like, or the way it also made him vomit that he didn't like. He was not yet eight months old and couldn't tell us, and never had I been more aware that we couldn't tell him anything either. We couldn't explain to him that we were doing all of these unpleasant things to him because it would make him feel better and because we loved him.

He cried. He fought. He struggled.

So did we. After giving him his medication, Henry and I were both in foul moods, and I was the softy. I was wavering. Did we really need to give him this medication? Giving it to him was traumatic. How would he not hate us by the end of ten days? Ten days. How would we be able to do this to our son twice a day for ten days?

Henry stood strong and solid like the oak that he was. Yes, we did need to give him his medication. Ear infections were painful and could get worse if not treated. The cough syrup would help. Oliver didn't understand because he was a baby. He didn't know any better. We were adults. That's why we do it anyway. It would be OK. Would you prefer he keep seizing up and stop breathing?

After the first dose of each bottle, we continued to examine him. The side effects of the medication, though rare, included death. And when death was included, the word "rare" did little to comfort me. We kept exposing his chest to look for rashes or color changes. We watched his breathing to see if it was speeding up or slowing down (as if we'd really be able to recognize something wrong in his breathing with him already being so congested from being sick).

He remained normal though tired, low energy, and still fussy. My mother rolled her eyes constantly. "He was fine, and he still is. He didn't need the medicine in the first place," she said as she went out to her yoga class.

Oliver didn't sleep well. Laying him down seemed to allow the phlegm to fill his lungs, and the coughing spurts would startle and wake him. Half the time he was able to settle, and the other half of the time, the coughing led to vomiting. Each heavy vomiting event was followed by Henry and I strategizing how and when and how much to feed him. Sleep training had become but a distant memory, and by the morning, we were completely defeated.

After the first day and night of medicine, I came downstairs to greet my family. It was as if I had entered the wrong house. My mother was making breakfast for my other three sisters. Cosmic was in a white silk robe with one knee bent so that her foot rested on the ledge of the chair. She looked like a morning goddess. Angelica's face was done up for the day with a full face of makeup, though there were no plans to leave the house quite yet. Amelia was still in sweats, but her radiant skin told me the long-lost story of a night of nine hours of sleep.

Henry was still trying to get a few minutes of sleep, so I sat there holding an awake Oliver. He had thrown up throughout the night, and the medication was also giving him diarrhea, so he was in his third outfit in the last eight hours.

I had always known the first Christmas with Oliver wouldn't convince any of my sisters to join me in the childbearing life I had chosen, but I had never imagined that it would remove any doubt about their choices for a childless life. If anything, I pictured our baby giving them an experience that was pleasantly neutral when it came to any birthing decision. Yet here I was, causing the concrete of a life with never having children to set and dry for the rest of my family. I sat there for a few moments with my scraggly hair tucked behind my ears. My itchy throat burning under my chin. My fingers jittery from forgetting to eat dinner while still offering Oliver my boob whenever his mouth opened even the slightest.

Angelica offered to hold Oliver. I obliged. My mother slid eggs onto a couple of plates for me and Henry.

"Did you not sleep at all?" she asked. "Where is Henry? Isn't he up?"

Most hours that I thought would be spent playing Spades with my sisters, lounging on the couches, asking and answering fun and fantastical questions that matched the energy of a Would You Rather? game, or going out to eat were actually spent cooped up in our room with Oliver, who didn't have the energy to venture far from his place of sleep. Neither did we.

It was only the third day since Oliver had been to urgent care when Henry started to feel unusually tired. In the night, he picked up an identical cough to our son. By the morning, he had lost most of his voice, only speaking (and wincing) when absolutely necessary. By day four, the intense fatigue and body aches had swept over my body. Both of us followed our son into his misery.

By the fourth night, I felt as if I had been thrown back into the nights that felt impossible. The first nights following Oliver's birth—when I was forced to fight sleep off to watch his chest rise and fall. When I woke up from sporadic sleeping pockets by the sound of my infant's cough, I raised my head into a small up-dog position to make sure it was just a cough, and that he wasn't covered in his own vomit or had seized up again.

On the fifth day, Henry and our "careless whisper fights" had lost their whisper. Suddenly, we were at each other's (sore) throats, and communication had faltered terribly. Jokes were offensive to the receiver, matter-of-fact comments were interrupted with insults, and our approach to caring for a sick Oliver changed every other second. Just administering medicine morning and night—the two most stressful events of the day—started with uncertainty and guaranteed a fight: Should we lay him down and give him the liquid or sit him up? Should we do it fast and get it over with or little by little to not upset his tummy? Should we mix it with chocolate syrup, or try it in breast milk, or just administer it on its own?

We never fully decided, so Oliver won most battles, swatting the medicine away as we both half-heartedly restrained him from this seemingly evil task we were performing. When we declared the deed was done excitedly, we bit our lips wondering how much of each carefully measured dose he was actually consuming.

There was no time or energy to talk through our feelings or arguments. There was no patience left to make a hand squeeze mean what it needed to in the little silences we had. We couldn't stand each other. In the moments I had time to think about things other than Oliver's health, like when I was walking to get the bottle of medicine or put it away, or rinsing out my pump, or peeing, I couldn't help but think of the growing number of divorces that had been popping up that year. None of them finalized, but among our friends and family, young couples—couples our age and with children—were splitting. Fred and Jessica. Danny and Jeff. Ashley and Graham. It was hard to not think about that and feel the pressure of it all when my communication with Henry felt like it had been broken down—no, obliterated—by a child's head cold and ear infection.

On the seventh day, my mother and sisters had all left

to go to a studio Angelica had rented out for family photos. I had showered, hoping we'd be feeling good enough to go, but we were a ways away from a full recovery. Oliver seemed more energetic, but his cough still made my heart stop. Henry was in the midst of the storm —in the worst of it all. I was probably just a day behind Henry.

With the house to ourselves, it was quiet. Oliver fell asleep seconds after the garage door closed, and Henry followed. With a headache and sore throat that wouldn't let me join them in slumber, I crept quietly downstairs so as not to wake them. I put on a kettle of hot water and prepared a cup of tea. After squeezing an entire bottle of honey into my cup, I paused for a moment. No shuffling. No shifting. Quiet. Oliver and Henry were both still asleep.

I walked out to the back porch and shut the door. Sitting on the little wooden chair with a small accent table, I took a sip of my tea. It was sweet on my tongue, soothing on my throat. I looked out at the bits of nature that had made their way into my mother's backyard and beyond. Blackbirds on the telephone pole. Leafless trees that were still months away from a first and tiny bloom. The chill of the wind and the weak warmth of the winter sun.

I thought about the moments in my past life, before Oliver was born, that this moment resembled. For example, I wasn't rushing through a cup of tea. I was sipping. Slowly. I was also noticing things that I wouldn't when multitasking, like the color of the clouds that surrounded the sun and the crooks of the branches of the trees. I had no time limit. No direction. No task to check off in this free time I had with Henry and Oliver passed out.

It reminded me of when I used to walk the cities I lived in. Whether it was Brooklyn, or Oakland, or Orlando, or Eugene, I used to go out in the day and walk with no destination. I made stops. Pastry shops. Cafés. Coffee carts. Park benches. Shady trees. I sometimes put in earphones. I sometimes spoke with strangers. But most of the time I just listened. I spent hours out there, in the world, on my own. Exploring. Unattached to the home I had started my walks from. It was an activity that I would have never quite associated with freedom at the time. At the time, I had felt more lonely, wistful, lost—but still happy.

I took another sip of tea. The world outside seemed to be speaking to me. It was as if the world had beckoned me into the backyard to say, "It's OK. It's safe to come back."

Breastfeeding had tethered me to my child. My fears had caused me to micromanage my husband around and with our son. My anxiety had me on standby when I was only inches away from our little human. The burden I carried made it too much to carry anything else.

It was at this very moment that I realized I had to make a change. It must get better. I had to get better. I didn't have to walk for hours in a new neighborhood in the city alone. But I needed to start inching toward some of the things I needed as an individual, which also required me to start inching away from my firstborn and only son.

I needed to take tea on the porch when we returned to our own home in the city. I needed to say yes to lunch with Alex. I needed to go to the 7:00 a.m. yoga class. I needed to stay in the bath and finish the page I was on, even if Oliver was crying. Because Henry was there, and

Henry needed me to return to the world too. Maybe he needed that even more than I did.

Yes, we three were sick, but we were breaking in other ways, and the illnesses were simply exposing the cracks. It wouldn't get better until I realized what I felt out on that porch. It must get better. I must get better. In small increments, I must act.

After about half an hour on the porch, I went inside. I hadn't had that much time to myself in nearly eight months and had run out of things to do. It was still quiet on the stairs. They were still asleep. So, I wandered my mother's house like it was a neighborhood in a familiar city. Finally, I heard my baby's cry, and I returned upstairs —consciously forcing myself to pace my steps when my heart was telling me to run up the stairs two at a time.

I opened the door and saw Henry holding our little one. Oliver's cries were still there, but they were not as strong as they had been a minute earlier. Oliver was too distracted by the whiskers on Henry's face to really commit to the cries. Oliver quieted when he saw my face.

I walked to my husband, and our eyes met without hostility for the first time in a week. He kissed me on the forehead.

I took Oliver into my arms instinctually, getting ready to feed him. I sat on the bed, and Oliver latched. Henry sat beside me and rested his head on my shoulder. We felt close all of a sudden. With my child physically connected to my body once again, I already felt so far away from that feeling, from the outside world, from my life as an individual. But I took deep breaths and reminded myself what the world had told me over tea: it's safe to come back.

29

THE HARDEST, THE BEST, AND THE UNEXPECTED

I often get this question from friends. I thought I would answer it here as well since you and I are friends just the same now.

The Hardest

Breastfeeding. It was by far the most challenging part of the first few months of Oliver's life. Of course, that's also what I think has given me some of the most precious memories. Looking down in the wee hours of the morning to see my little boy gulping milk is a favorite hobby of mine. Sometimes his eyes are closed, and he is feeding and dreaming at once. Sometimes he's awake and will pause to unlatch, look up at me, and smile. It's almost as if he is saying, "Thanks for the milk, Mom. You're the best." Though it pains me that Henry will never experience this firsthand, I find it makes the practice feel even more sacred. This activity will only be shared between us, and that is special.

However, breastfeeding continues to be the most challenging, and the reason I mention breastfeeding before lack of sleep is because breastfeeding gets in the way of sleeping. If I weren't feeding my child directly from my chest, sleeping would probably be a lot easier at this point —nine months post Oliver's birth. But I still struggle with hard, full breasts in the middle of the night. I still struggle when my breasts fill and leak when he cries in the night. I still struggle without being able to tag team milk feeds with Henry (as I stopped pumping a couple of months ago). It takes its toll on me and all of our sleep.

The honorable mention in this category is the worry. There will never be a moment when I don't worry for him, want the best for him, fear the worst for him. It hurts to just think of the possibilities of the many things that can go wrong in an ordinary day, and if I stop and dwell, the anxiety can be crippling. Good thing there is not much time to stop and dwell...

The Best

It's intangible. As soon as I set out to write this book, I knew it. I knew I was attempting the impossible. There is no way to encapsulate the wonder, and awe, and adoration I feel for my baby. There is no way to explain the love I feel for Henry when I see him standing over the crib and reaching for Oliver's toes. There is no way to fully process or articulate this joy. It's overwhelming, immense, staggering, but I am failing at communicating it here with words.

Maybe if I go back to what was the hardest...

When the worry becomes so great, I feel paralyzed. When the idea of losing Henry or Oliver—this family of mine—intrusively makes its way into my brain, I whisk it away by reframing all of the apprehension. I go from:

What if I lose Henry or Oliver? What if something bad happens to them? How will I go on?

to:

I have been given a family and life so marvelous that I now have something to lose. And what life is worth living if we didn't worry every now and then if we lost it?

This is a happy, fulfilling life. It's something I care about. Something I work for and protect. Something I value and share. Something I am so grateful for that it hurts to have because it makes me so... vulnerable.

The best things come in all shapes and sizes. Oliver's laugh is contagious. His boogers astound me. His toes are wondrous. The way the drool glistens on his chin, so innocent. Henry's sound effects with plush toys are opening up a new person inside of him. One I have never met before. My husband's storybook voice is something I look forward to just as much as Oliver does each evening. The details in my life feel incredible.

I sometimes find myself outside, walking among the bushes and trees. I'm holding Oliver, and he reaches out to pinch a leaf between his fingers. His lips are out in an O of curiosity, and his eyes are transfixed on the waxy, green surface. It's then, when looking at him, that I wonder when the last time I held a leaf in my hand just to study the foliage of a tree was. When was the last time I studied the texture of nature? Once again, Oliver and his youth are renewing the wonders of the world to his old, rusting mother.

The Unexpected

For me, it was relationships. After Oliver arrived, every relationship in my life changed. Even before he arrived, really. My marriage jumped through one hundred levels in twenty milliseconds once Oliver was born, and it now looks so different from what it did. My relationship with my direct family spaced out and quieted down so much more than I was prepared for. My relationship with my husband's side of the family improved—I now have the topic of children to fall back on in any situation with my in-laws. The childfree friends that stayed in my life are now more dear, and the new friends I've made with children are my lifesavers.

It takes a village to raise a child. But we don't live in villages anymore. We don't know thy neighbor anymore. In today's world, you have to create your village and maintain it. You have to cultivate it and sustain it. It's hard, but the alternative is unfeasible.

Finally, my relationship with myself. Ah, yes. It has changed too. I have far more respect for myself. I have witnessed what I'm capable of and now understand I am still yet to reach my limits. I know that my strength runs deep and that, in fact, my limits are so much greater than I ever imagined. I've found that it has been necessary to prioritize myself and my needs and have a better understanding of what putting myself first looks like—even when it's inconvenient for everyone involved. What must be sacrificed in order to do so, and why that's OK. I value myself so much more, as well as the community that continues to support me. I know when it's OK to be spread thin, and I know what it is to bend and also to break.

Every relationship has changed, and it was not something I anticipated. I mourn some of my connections; I nourish others with determination; and all of them, I cherish and revere in different ways.

30

THE ACHE

I found myself doing something I never would have thought I would do. Before having Oliver, I had heard about calcification: jewelry made out of breastmilk. Just the thought of wearing jewelry made of that ingredient—even my own—made me queasy. As a marketer, I understood that there was an audience for everything. I wasn't a part of that audience.

Well, I wasn't when I was pregnant.

Today is the third day Oliver has not had any breastmilk. He has drunk only whole milk and water. He is thirteen months old and asleep for the night—sleeping twelve hours each night consistently. He and Henry have an understanding among topics such as diaper changes, snack time, and taking time on each page as Oliver tries to fly through thirty board books in three minutes. I, mother of Oliver, wife to Henry, am sitting in the corner of the living room, secretly scrolling through a page of breastmilk jewelry heirlooms. I'm so embarrassed by this feeling I have about weaning from breastfeeding that I'm tempted to delete my browsing history . . . That is, after I decide if I want an oval-designed jewel or smaller circle, and on gold or silver.

The transition has been easy for Henry, who has wanted to wean since Oliver turned six months old. He's found Oliver's dependency on my nipples to soothe himself somewhat frustrating. Oliver often wanted the boob, and it when I was working, it was hard for Henry to manage, especially since Henry is the primary caretaker of our son—which also made it harder to fight him on weaning. I lost the battle, and after tireless arguments that hadn't been fully resolved around sleep training, I didn't have the fight to demand a second year of breastfeeding.

The days used to start with me greeting Oliver in the morning, picking him up, changing him, and then bringing him to our bed, where I would let him feed while I closed my eyes, cuddling close and tracing the features of my son from his bronze curls and dimpled elbows to toes that often twinkled while he ate. Often Henry found the heel of our son and squeezed or the rosy cheek and tickled. There is no warmth like that warmth.

Now, with this transition, Henry wakes up to beat Oliver's wakefulness. He prepares a cup of milk in a silicone cup and straw (we skipped the bottle) with a cloth or bib since Oliver is a messy but enthusiastic drinker. Then Henry walks past our bedroom to get to Oliver's, picks him up, changes him—I hear the good mornings and greetings of the morning—and Henry quickly walks past our bedroom to get to the kitchen area as I hide under the covers. I hide so Oliver isn't tempted by my breasts, and I hide so I'm not tempted to intercept Henry's path myself. (I never knew how strong this urge would be.)

I compare myself to a vampire and that age-old frenzy they are sent into when they smell blood. When I see

Oliver and notice any signs of hunger—he signs milk, he whines, he crawls onto me, and lifts or pulls at my shirt—the desire to nourish him overpowers me. The want to feel relief that comes from his hunger and my full breast is strong. The ache to literally connect to myself, my eyes closed and arms circled around him, is unbearable.

I've said goodnight in the common area to Oliver before Henry puts him down—normally an activity I managed the majority of the time since I was unavailable during work. Bedtimes were rituals I shared with my son. The click of the humidifier, the sound of the air filter, the gargle of the sound machine. The select pages, torn and bent, were read religiously. The signs for "sleep," "goodnight," and "I love you," were learned through muscle memory. This was sacred.

Between full breasts, Oliver's yearning for a nightcap, and simply the desire to be peaceful and still with my ever-climbing, always-waddling son—I couldn't put myself in a room of temptation, or I would break my promise to Henry. I would let him down by letting down. So, I missed the beginning and ending of days with Oliver.

As I stand in the shower, letting the steaming, hot water rain on my breasts, I'm reminded of the first two months (or was it three?) of Oliver's life when my engorged breasts felt like blistered boils on my chest. When walking or even lying on my side caused my breasts to pulse in a raw, internally sunburnt kind of way. These showers are where I self-express, watching the milk travel in unique spurts to the drain. I grow resentful of the waste of perfectly good breastmilk. I feel angry toward Henry. I hit the tile semi-aggressively with a fist.

I've tried to lean on other mothers. How did weaning go for them? How did they refuse their children? How did they move on? But not a single one I've spoken to can relate to me. They all were forced or chose to feed their children formula not too long after birth. "I dried up at seven months," one of my friends said. I felt guilty because I envied her. It would be so much easier if my body stopped. If I didn't have a choice. I know that sounds selfish and inconsiderate to those who don't have a choice, but I'm feeling rather selfish right now—and quite vulnerable.

It turns out that even though breastfeeding has been one of the most incredibly hard things I've dealt with in these last twelve months, it has been the best. I mourn the time I held Oliver to feed him just like I mourn the milk that flows down my shower drain. Perhaps this is harder as well because Henry and I are not aligned. I don't feel seen or understood by him. I just feel like this loving feeling is a blocker for him, and I have to choose between Henry, Oliver, and myself. Those choices always make me suffer because it means I am truly alone in my decision and its results.

Tonight, day three and night three of just milk and water for Oliver, I was forced to work late. When I walked into the kitchen searching for my baby, he was fast asleep. I had missed his bedtime. I had missed the pain of deferring bedtime to Henry. Though some moments of parenthood—the tired moments that feel impossible—seem to last for great masses of time, there are moments, precious moments, filled with emotions that no book I'll ever write will come close to capturing. Those moments sometimes feel like they slip away when I close my eyes for the shortest second. My lungs will never take a deep enough breath to inhale all there is in this new life of parenting. I'll never have enough of my Oliver. I'll never have rocked him to sleep enough. I'll never have rolled and giggled with him enough. I'll never have fed him enough while his tummy kissed mine.

So, I guess on this Monday night, a gold-filled oval ring—a keepsake of this cherished ache—in my shopping cart will have to be enough to at least get me to tomorrow.

31

IF YOU CHOOSE

If you choose to have children, I have nothing to tell you. You are you. I am me. Here is what I can tell me. It's not all that I can tell me, but it's all that I can tell me before my baby wakes from his nap, so it will have to do:

Do everything you want to do before you have the baby. Eat at the twelve-course restaurant. Do the fifteen-hour flight to Tokyo. Do nothing all day for a week until your brains melt into cheese dip. Take the salsa classes, or the jujitsu classes, or the cooking classes. Do the weekend trip on the long, winding roads. Pay for the bath before the massage and get the facial after. I don't care for sports, but if you do, fly to the big game. Paint your face. Do it all. And when the next chapter of your life begins with a little one, you will miss the rich life you lived, you will mourn it, but you won't regret not having had it.

If you decide to have a partner when having a baby, make sure you choose the right person. I have my strange ways of knowing that it is easier to go it alone than with the wrong person—as impossible as that situation may seem. Do everything you can to choose best. I know that's so hard to do. It's so hard to know. So, I'll leave it at this. Find someone kind. Someone patient. Someone reliable. Someone whose strengths balance your weaknesses. Someone honest. Someone who can do hard things on their own. Someone who doesn't think they're better than you, and just as importantly, someone who doesn't think you're better than them. Someone equal. Ultimately, choose wisely.

Arrange help. You can hope for a good, chill baby, but you'll need to plan for more difficult arrangements. How will food be making it to the table? How will chores get done if you're on baby duty? Who is watching the baby? What if you have your baby earlier than expected? Maybe your baby is lucky and has able-bodied grandparents that live close by and adore your baby. Maybe your friend Becky has vowed to help and can't wait to be an auntie. (Don't count on Becky.) Make sure you know who is going to come and help on weekdays while you recover, while you work, while you rest, while you sleep, while you do the laundry. Only depend on those serious enough to commit to a weekly schedule with hours that you can depend on. (Hint: this will most likely require hiring someone that you pay to make sure this is a reliable arrangement.) Also, look into postpartum doulas. I did not have one when I had Oliver, but I will have one for my next child. Henry doesn't believe this is necessary, but I don't care. Again, hope for the good, chill baby, but plan for the colicky baby. Plan for the preterm baby. Make sure you and the village that will take care of you—whether it's out of love or because you are paying them—is ready and expectations are set.

Finally, know how you're going to afford a baby and all of the unexpected things (emergencies included!) that may come with one. You can never be fully ready, but with all things baby prep, be as ready as you can. Finances are no exception.

32

I CALL HIM

Gargoyle for the screeching.
    Lovebug for the reaching.
    Chubs for the thighs.
    Cherub for the eyes.
    My Guy for the laughs.
    My Guyyyyyyyy for the giggles.
    BFG for the growing.
    Olympic Athlete for the wiggles.

Little Terror for the wailing.
    The monk for the proper in and exhaling.
    Squishy face for the cheeks.
    The scholar for when he speaks.
    The whole world and all that matters.
    The warmth, the love, the light.
    The only thing that gets me up,
    And keeps me up at night.

33

MAMA

I'm standing in front of a mirror performing an unusual activity: observing myself. This is actually quite rare for me. I only stand in front of a mirror when multitasking. It might be flossing or brushing my teeth. Maybe plucking one of the two chin hairs that have grown in the same exact place since I turned twenty-two. Or perhaps applying a prescription-strength cream to a rash near my hairline that showed up about three weeks after I gave birth to my son. It flares up when I'm stressed.

Honestly, I find myself multiple times a week out and about with the sudden realization that I haven't even looked in a mirror that day. This is most likely because I was performing the hygienic tasks usually done in front of a mirror while doing something else—cue me brushing my teeth while feeding my son breakfast in his highchair.

But not now. In this moment, I'm standing with my hands free, and I see my reflection. But what I really see is my hair. It's looking like Merida's hair from the movie *Brave*. My hair is long—growing down to my breasts—but it's curly also. So, if it were straightened, it would most likely hover over the small of my back. My hands can't help themselves as I look at my locks. My fingers are hungry for the texture, and they dig into my scalp near my hairline, where I notice I have four thick braids layered into the many, many strands of hair. I see all of the things I've always wanted my appearance to represent in this newfound human foliage: abundance, fun, the wild.

I turn this way and that. I spin around, allowing my eyes only to leave my sight for a second. For the first time since I was combing through the balding areas on my head after I had Henry, I am entertaining myself only by looking at my hair. I'm really looking, and I am incredibly vibrant with my loose, bouncing curls. I tell myself I will finally commit to learning how to do my hair so I can braid it, and bun it, and curl and straighten it as I please. I think of Henry and my son, and chuckle at the idea of him yanking a rich coil of my hair while I change his diaper. I gush at the idea of accidentally catching a strand of hair on fire while leaning over to get a whiff of what my husband is cooking over our gas stove. I think about the watering eyes of my husband when I turn my head too fast, causing my hair to whip his eyes as if to punish him for trying to follow the abrupt changing of my gaze. More hair, more problems—and I welcome the problems.

It's time to leave the mirror and head toward my family. To show my husband this amazing transformation I have somehow made. To finally feel that womanly, feminine connection to "mother" that I felt I was lacking when I looked at all the photos of myself interacting with my baby. No more short-haired, balding, awkward tufts. No. Now I have motherly hair. I have Mother Nature hair. I finally look how I feel on the inside. I'm a jungle. I'm always growing, progressing, pushing onward. I'm messy, flexible, elastic. I'm mother.

I wake up.

My baby is babbling. His new favorite word is "yellow-yellow-yellow." My head is pounding, and the pressure of my sinuses from the second cold we've caught in three weeks is making it feel as if the ceiling is resting on top of me. But my baby has alerted the mother within me, and I sit up anyway. It is cold in Salt Lake now, even inside, and especially in the greeting of morning. So, I pull on my robe that rests on top of the bed covers and wrap it tightly around my bare chest and shoulders.

We are in a kind of makeshift Jack-and-Jill situation in our home, so that to get to my baby, I must walk through a bathroom. I feel the cold tile on my feet, awakening my own bodily needs. I pee before I open the door on the opposite wall. He hears me from the bathroom and immediately responds to the sounds of activity. His babbling becomes stressed, whiny. No formed words in these sounds, but I hear the translation clear as day: Where is mother? Why is she awake and not tending to me? His noises pull on the strings of my soul, but he isn't crying yet. It took eighteen months, but I have learned not to rush (too much) and give myself the time that I need. Time I need to breathe. Time I need to get my bearings. Time I need to pee, goddammit.

Where is mother? he gurgles again.

After drying my hands from the flow of cold water, I open the door. I can only see the dark silhouette of my child.

I turn briefly to see the bathroom mirror for a moment, momentarily recalling my dream. I see my true reflection in the darkness that can only be created through the leftover light of a cold winter morning in Utah, and I see myself. Really see myself.

My eyes are puffy. My skin damp from the morning oils. My robe is inside out. My mouth is a thin line, seconds before I turn it into a smile for my son. I see my hair. It is short. Thin. Fine. Still disappearing every day.

Today, the stark contrast from my reflection in my dream makes my barren scalp somewhat painful to see. The hair that does exist is lightly matted and pointed in a zigzag of directions, reminding me of how Calvin looks after Hobbes pounces on him when he returns from school.

Mother, you're here! My son's sounds that were on the verge of a cry turn into a relieved, breathy laughter.

With my eyes lingering on my hair, I finally pull my attention away and look at what's in front of me. I don't have the curly hair from my dream. I don't even have the thick, South Korean hair I might have had if this were a different life. I just have some hair. I have the hair of a malnourished boy. I am not Mother Nature. So, I correct him in this telepathic conversation.

I'm just Mom.

Even so, he lets go of the crib railing and stretches his hands toward me.

I pick him up and examine my boy. Alert. Ready. Eyes wide. Tight, coiled curls extending from his head in every which way. When it comes to hair, he did not get the curls from me, but he certainly got the disheveled morning shape from me.

About now in my dream, he'd be playing with a curl that fell loosely on my shoulder. In this reality, he decides to promptly attempt to fill my mouth with his fingers—an awkward power move that I acknowledge. I reach for his hand, envelop them in my unusually large hands, and breathe warmth into them. These mornings are cold when sleep is still thawing.

"Mama," he says out loud, clear and undeniable.

It's a compromise. An offer that I unconditionally accept.

"Mama," I agree.

34

WOULD YOU?

Oliver was a week shy of five months old when I received a memorable text from Henry's sister. It was a photo. She was standing by the window of the hospital with her husband beside her, and her babe—who was born only eleven hours earlier—was sleeping in her arms. I saw the pull-out chair behind them. The door to the little bathroom. The sheets on the hospital bed. The recovery room.

I felt joy recalling my own recovery room after having Oliver at three in the morning. And strange. Unexpectedly, I felt a longing to be back in the recovery room with a small, buggy-eyed newborn with half the lung capacity for a full cry. Before I could stop myself, I spoke.

"I want another one."

Henry looked at me. He nodded once as if I had said we need to get more bananas the next time we go to the grocery store. "Make it a girl," he said.

Henry continued reading Milton on the couch. I stared back at the image of the couple on my phone. The mother with a puffy but pleased face, and the father with a stringy, sleepless twinkle in his eye.

Did I really want to be in the recovery room again?

The bottom of my breasts now semi-permanently stuck to the rib cage underneath them, and I felt their heavy plop every time I took a step down the stairs. When I heard Oliver's cry, my nipples pulsated and wet like the whistling spouts of a teapot. I had an obligation every two and a half hours that tethered me to a fourteen-and-a-half-pound body that depended on me. My nights, once long and slumberous, were now endlessly interrupted—and frequently.

What was worse was that I was guilty of finding myself waking Oliver to feed, missing him, and needing him more than he missed and needed me when the night felt long and restless. There was a ridge in my vagina where I tore as Oliver started this life of his, and though it doesn't hurt, I still am afraid to press too hard against it. Once a champion of pull-ups, doing eleven in a row at my best, I can no longer do even one. And though I take him with me where I can, there are some places he cannot come—my job, my appointments—my calendar revolves around him. I—who have never had to do any unpleasant math before a purchase—have created a 529 account for him as well as now budgeting my monthly spending. The worries of *What will I eat for lunch?* or, *Should I go on that vacation in the fall?* have been taken over by a constant, anxiety-ridden question of, *Is my child still breathing?*

Did I really want another one?

I have read exactly seven books on child sleep psychology, sleep training, and the science of sleep. I have highlighted both the *Mayo Clinic's Guide to a Healthy Pregnancy* and *What to Expect When Expecting* (the most recent edition). I researched strollers for about thirty-two hours too long. I have spoken to at least five lactation consultants and three pediatricians on breastfeeding and growth charts alone. I have taken twelve weeks of prenatal yoga. I have taken four virtual classes on newborn and infant care. I check the American Academy of Pediatrics on a monthly basis for any news or updates on things like safe sleep, breastfeeding recommendations, and COVID guidance. I have become certified in infant CPR and watch refresher videos every two months. I have watched approximately twenty videos of six-month-olds to two-year-olds transitioning from breast milk to solid foods. I have downloaded a sleep, feed, and diaper app that I use religiously and have forced Henry to adopt as well. And I have spent far too much money on baby and mother things, of which only half I actually use.

Not many mothers will admit it, and I admit, the longer I'm a mother, the more I see Oliver grow, the less I'm willing to admit it too. Having a baby was hard. Not only was it hard, some parts were miserable, nearly unbearable. There was the first-trimester nausea—which was long and drawn out—to the excruciating contractions that were powerful and relentless. The sleepless nights that stretch out whatever makes up my soul to such a thinness I tremble just thinking about it. And the worry. Going through it all only to worry your heart away over your child. Is he getting enough to eat? Is he growing as he should be? Is he breathing while he lies in that crib? Will SIDS make him a statistic? What if he chokes on something? What if he bumps his head? What if he has RSV? Oh, the worry.

Is it just that the baby is cute? Is that what it is? Is that why I dare say I want another? Is Oliver's button nose and sweet chocolate eyes what draw me in?

Sitting on the couch, I heard him coo from the crib.

Automatically, I stood up and went to him. There he lay on his back, his eyes wandering until they noticed he was not alone. He saw me. His head tilted. I leaned forward and smiled. He smiled back. He reached out to me with both hands, and I obliged first by lowering my head. His fingers, small but strong, touched my face, felt my joy, learned my love.

Some of my braver, more curious friends have asked me directly. *Would you do it all over again? You know. Have a baby. If you knew how hard it actually was?*

There's a part of me from my past that wants to tell my friends: Run. Don't have a baby. Never be pregnant. Always sleep when you want and for as long as you want. Never expand your belly unless it is for more dessert.

And perhaps they *should* run.

As for me, I've come too far. I now know the weight and warmth of my Oliver in my arms, asleep on my chest. I know the tired but unlimited kisses of my Henry, the quiet gasps he takes when he remembers his own innocence through the eyes of our son. I know the strength of my body, the power of my intuition, and the ocean-like capacity of my love. I cannot look back. There's too much to look forward to.

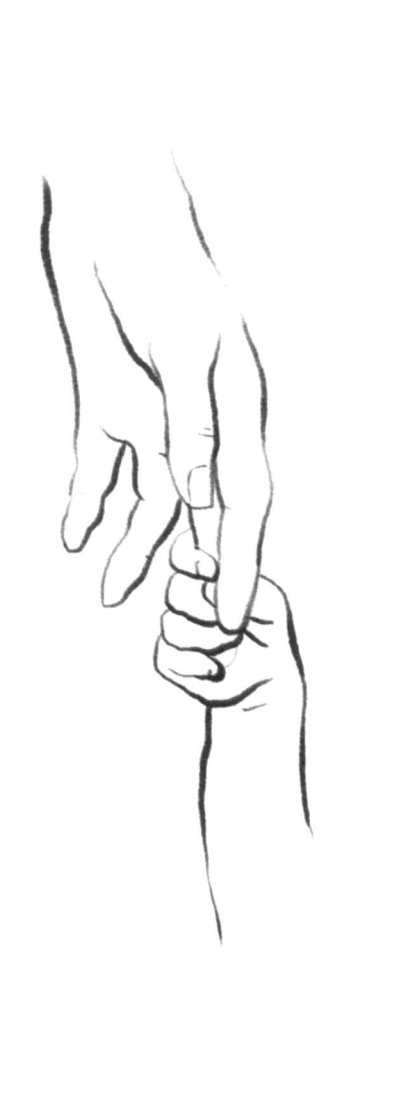

ABOUT THE AUTHOR

Jade Kim Monsen is a Korean American writer who lives in Salt Lake City, Utah and has a strange love for the color green. When she's not reading or writing or brainstorming, she's working as a marketer for her day job, talking to anyone who will listen about the ups and downs of motherhood, or spending time with her husband, son, and two dogs at the park. Literally. Like that's all she does.

www.JadeKimMonsen.com
@JadeKimMonsen

Subscribe to the JadeKimWrites newsletter for personal blog posts, book updates, and more.

ABOUT THE ILLUSTRATOR

Rachel Sierra grew up moving all over the Caribbean and Central America, and travel has been a central part of her life. As a self-taught artist and multidisciplinary creative, when she's not painting in her studio, you'll find her getting lost in a new project, or at the beach surfing. She has a small family, and is a new mom. She is endlessly exploring what it looks like to embrace the archetype of a creative mother, and has yet to see how it will continue to be reflected in her work. She is driven to document life in anyway - whether that's by painting, taking film photos, or designing book covers!

Rachelsierraart.com

ACKNOWLEDGMENTS

I want to thank my husband, David, for taking on more than he should so I a follow my dreams. His belief in me and support for me has made this first book possible.

All five of my sisters have listened to me talk about my book(s) and offered support in their own way. I'd especially like to thank Meg for her recording herself sobbing after finishing Ava's Socks. I also want to thank her for teaching me to "just ask" and also for teaching me to be direct and kind—so those hard conversations can be had.

I'd also like to thank my mother, for her own milk and blood.

I owe so much to my creative writing professor in college, Tony Watkins. It is an amazing feeling when someone you look up to believes in you. Thank you so much for calling me out of the blue to ask, "Are you still writing?"

I'd also like to thank my readers. Some of you have been here since the beginning. Some of you are newer to my words. All of you have taken the time to sit and read in a world where we have no time. Your words of encouragement and connection have been the whisper in my ear all this time telling me not to give up.

Thank you all so much. My dreams don't come true without you.

THE STREET TEAM

You know who you are, but I also want to thank each of you personally for your support.

The Street Team:
- Alex Giddens
- Anita Lee
- Ashley Roosa
- Austin Miller
- Dani Mortimer
- David Candland Monsen
- Dia Frampton
- Gian Florendo
- Huaning "Wendy" Wang
- Justin Moss
- Mark and Jessica Hollingshead
- Matt Aquino
- Michael F. Ballman
- Rosemary Asuka-LeCroy
- Sunhee Kim Frampton
- Taylor Miller

Made in United States
Troutdale, OR
07/09/2025